Dark Prairie

Dark Prairie

John D. Nesbitt

FIVE STAR
A part of Gale, Cengage Learning

GALE
CENGAGE Learning

Detroit • New York • San Francisco • New Haven, Conn • Waterville, Maine • London

GALE
CENGAGE Learning

LIBRARY OF CONGRESS CATALOGING-IN-PUBLICATION DATA

Nesbitt, John D.
Dark prairie / John D. Nesbitt. — First edition.
pages cm
ISBN 978-1-4328-2750-2 (hardcover) — ISBN 1-4328-2750-2 (hardcover)
1. Cowboys—Fiction. I. Title.
PS3564.E76D38 2013
813'.54—dc23 2013008088

First Edition. First Printing: July 2013
Find us on Facebook– https://www.facebook.com/FiveStarCengage
Visit our website– http://www.gale.cengage.com/fivestar/
Contact Five Star™ Publishing at FiveStar@cengage.com

Printed in Mexico
1 2 3 4 5 6 7 17 16 15 14 13

For Robert Roripaugh

Chapter One

The man named Dunbar came to the town of Winsome in the late summer of the year. I first saw him when he rode out to the Little Six, looking for work as a ranch hand. Our country was broad, rolling grassland, not nearly as flat up close as it looked from a distance, and a rider could appear on the landscape as if he had just materialized. That was how Dunbar showed up—a tall man with a bushy mustache as dark as his high-crowned hat. He was riding a blue roan and leading a buckskin that carried his bed and other gear.

The day had worn on to early evening, so the land lay in patches of shadow, starting with the darkest shade at Decker Rim, fifteen miles away, and flecking the country wherever the ground rose or fell. It looked like a different country at dusk than it did during sunny summer days—or winter days also, for that matter. In sunlight or shade, either one, the basin was quiet and still and isolated. Even in town, much less in the country, a person never heard a train, a rock crusher, a sawmill, or any other machine. It was the kind of place where people would say that nothing ever happened but the weather, but that wasn't quite true.

Dunbar came riding my way, a man and two horses moving in soft shadow with the darkening prairie in the background. As he came closer, I saw he had broad, full shoulders and a high chest. Closer still, I noticed his dark hair, eyes, and brows. I took him to be in his middle thirties, that prime of life that yet lay ahead of me. As he drew the roan to a stop, he struck me as one of those men of great strength and energy, with an almost animal-like vitality. He wore a charcoal-colored wool vest, and for a moment he reminded me of a large-antlered, husky deer that might have just emerged from a canyon along Decker Rim.

"Is this the way to the Little Six?" he asked.

"It sure is."

"Folks in town said I might find work there."

"Can't say. You'll have to talk to Hig. He's the owner."

"You work there, too, I take it?"

"That's right. I'll ride in with you if you like."

"Fine with me." He smiled.

I saw his gloved hand rise as he gave a tug on the lead rope, and as he put the blue roan into motion, I turned my horse and headed for the Little Six. Neither of us spoke as we rode across the grassland, where the gentle hills seemed to be settling into rest as the daylight faded by the minute.

I waited in the yard with the horses while Dunbar went in to talk to Higgins. A short while later, he came out of the house. Dusk had fallen, and his dark vest reminded me again of a buck deer.

He paused a couple of steps away from me, and his voice was clear and steady on the evening air. "Well, he hired me. He said you could show me where to put my horses. You're Grey, aren't you?"

"That's right. Grey Wharton."

He held out his hand. "I'm Dunbar."

"Pleased to meet you," I said as we shook hands. "I'll show you to the barn."

He nodded as he pulled his gloves onto his hands.

Once inside, I lit a lantern and hung it on a rafter. I unsaddled my horse and led him out the back door. When I got back,

Dunbar had unsaddled the roan and was untying the pack on the buckskin. He pulled on a lash rope, and the pack sagged loose and relaxed.

"How many fellas work here?"

"Four riders now, with you."

"Not many." He tossed the rope across the top of the pack.

"I expect he'll put on more for fall roundup."

Dunbar went around the back of the buckskin and stood on the off side. "It's all the same, I guess. I actually like it better workin' for a small outfit." He pulled the big round bedroll off the top of the pack and smiled in the lamplight. "Don't have to wait so long for chuck. How's the cook?"

"Oh, he's all right. I suppose you mean the grub. It's good."

He set the bedroll aside and took to picking at another knot on the pack. "That's what I meant. Doesn't matter too much who cooks it."

"Don't tell him that."

Dunbar smiled again. "Not in a hundred years."

I rode into town by myself the next day. With fall roundup still a month or six weeks away, and work not very pressing at the ranch, Hig sent me to town every two or three days. My main job on these trips was to fetch the mail, along with anything else he or Manfred the cook might need, but it was also understood that any news I picked up would be welcome as well.

I set out after noon dinner. The sun was high and warm, and the grass that had looked gray the evening before was shining in tones of pale yellow and tan. Here and there I saw small bunches of antelope, from two or three to seven or eight. When I came within a couple of hundred yards, they would flash the white of their rumps and bellies as they turned and wheeled away. From that distance, not a sound came. Closer in, grasshoppers whirred as my horse's hooves set down in a muffled clip-clop. A light breeze from the northwest brushed my face and cooled the perspiration on my forehead and scalp as I lifted my hat. Up above, I saw the white bottom of a prairie falcon as it drifted in the blue sky. The little world of Decker Basin seemed at peace.

The ride to town, being about ten miles, took close to two hours when I wasn't in a hurry. In good time I came to the line of hills that blocked the town from view. I followed the trail as always, through the gap, and then I saw the shiny surface of the pond and the town of Winsome beyond it.

The pond lay in a low spot, while the town sat on a level plain some fifty feet above it. I followed the trail downslope and into the bottom, along the east side of the pond where the earthen dam rose up on my left. It was not a big reservoir, as the surface of the pond, now that it was full, spread out over twenty acres, while the dike, as it appeared on this side, rose to about twelve feet at the highest. I had worked on the project, and although I had quit before it was finished, it always held an air of familiarity for me.

I followed the trail across the stone bridge that spanned the ditch. Up on my left, just above eye level, a smooth stream of water flowed out of the wooden headgate—a head of water, as the project men called it, about six feet wide and not much more than an inch deep. It poured through the gate, trickled down the rock-lined spillway, flowed under the bridge, and made its way down the ditch toward hayfields and a couple of truck gardens.

I took the short and not very steep climb up the slope on the other side, passing through a cutbank of whitish tan clay. Up on the level area, I turned and looked at the blue surface of the pond. Then I rode one block to the main street, turned where the livery stable sat on my left, and rode across the street to Fenn Fuller's mercantile and dry goods store. There I asked for the mail and found nothing. Fuller's clerk told me that his employer was "across the street," which was where I was expecting to go anyway.

The Whitepaw Saloon was the regular meeting place for a group of men I thought of as the council, and as such, it was a good place to pick up news or at least gossip. The council, which was not elected but assumed the role, consisted of four men who had the longest standing in town. They had all known my father and had been various kinds of friends with him, so they regarded me as a kind of nephew, and they welcomed me to draw up a chair and quaff a glass of beer. I did not take the welcome lightly, for it was not extended to the druggist, the barber, the milliner, or the latecomer who ran the general store.

I paused inside the door of the Whitepaw Saloon and let my eyes adjust. The first thing I settled on was the familiar sight of a stuffed bobcat standing in his usual place on a shelf that jutted out from the left side of the back wall. The animal had his head raised, and he held a white paw halfway to chest level and poised as if he was ready to take a swipe. From there my eyes moved to the lit area behind the bar. Above the wood-framed mirror hung a painting of an Indian warrior on his knees, straddling his enemy and holding a knife aloft. The conquest, or soon-to-be victim, had bare legs and was wearing sandals with thongs around his ankles. I guessed that the owner of the saloon, Lon Buckley, was proud of those two displays, as he kept them well lighted. I think they were meant to sustain the illusion that the Whitepaw was a place of danger and adventure, although it was easy enough for me to look at the rough boards of the back wall and remember what lay behind it—a storeroom of kegs and dark bottles, then an empty lot strewn with cans and clear bottles, and then empty air, hovering over the pond.

Three of the four council members were seated at a table. Fenn Fuller, who was the unofficial head of the group, sat in his usual place with his back to the bar. From that position he could see whoever came and went. As I walked in his direction, he tipped his head up and to one side and said, "Have a seat, boy."

I nodded, went around the post in back of him, and took a chair at his left. In less than a minute, Herb the bartender set a glass of beer in front of me. I exchanged greetings with Lon Buckley, the proprietor, and Al Redington, the butcher. Then I settled back in my chair, in my customary role of sitting at the edge and not barging in with comments.

Fenimore Fuller, or Fenn, was holding forth on a favorite topic. "I've said it before, and I'll probably say it again. You've got to get the attention of the right people. We've got water, and we're getting more water. If you can get someone to see that there'll be tons and tons of beans and corn and wheat, not to mention cattle and other livestock, they should be able to see that running a spur line here would be good business."

The other two nodded.

Fenn Fuller went on. "The more this town grows, the more we'll need—lumber, coal, hardware, dry goods, groceries, you name it. Sure, even wire and fence posts. Windmill parts."

The others nodded again.

"Sometimes it's just a matter of making connections."

Al Redington spoke. "Them that's got 'em seem to be puttin' 'em to their own use."

Fenn raised his eyebrows, and his bluish-gray eyes looked out through gold-rimmed spectacles. "Maybe he needs to be convinced, too. These things go hand in hand."

I knew they were referring to Ben Marston, who was building the bank and providing the backing for the water project.

Fenn let out a short breath and shook his head. "You've just got to get people to do things. You take something like this pond out here." He pointed his thumb over his shoulder. "He didn't lift a finger to get it going. You know who did. We did.

But once he saw Whipple could do the work, why, hell yes, he picked him up to do the big project. So that's why I say, we've got to convince someone." He reached for his glass of brandy and took a sip.

I drank from my glass and appreciated the cool, bitter taste. I wondered whether in a year from now the beer would be colder. One of the arguments for putting in the reservoir was that men could cut ice in the winter and store it. Fenn Fuller had spoken of building an ice house for a secondary business, but as far as I knew, he hadn't started one yet.

I gave a casual look his way. As so often happened, he seemed like a man I barely knew, even though I had known him since I was a little boy. He had filled out with the passing of time, and his ruddy cheeks suggested comfortable living. His reddish-gray hair was thinning on top, just as his red side-whiskers were running to silver. As he had not trimmed the whiskers in a while, he might remind a person of a fox in winter.

As I glanced over him, I thought he also dressed more carefully than he did when he and my father were young. He wore a tan suit with jacket, vest, and pants of lightweight wool, and always a dark brown tie. His bowler hat with the curled brim hung on the post behind his chair.

Fenn looked at me and smiled in his benevolent-uncle manner. "What's new, Grey? I heard someone was out your way lookin' for work."

"That's right. Hig put him on."

Fenn raised his eyebrows. "Aren't things kind of slow right now?"

"Might be at the moment."

Lon Buckley, who was a friend of Higgins, spoke up. "Oh, Hig knows what he's doin'. He'll have plenty of work for him before long."

"Sure," said Fenn. "Maybe he knows a good man when he

sees one, wants to keep him around." He smiled at me again. "How's cowpunchin'?"

"It's all right." I felt a small sinking of the spirits, but I was used to Fenn's patronizing manner. It went a ways back.

My father had said a few things that I remembered and heeded. One was that he was taking too long to die, which I didn't agree with but came to understand. When he was gone, there wasn't much for me to get by on. But I was old enough to work at jobs around town, and I didn't see where I had much room to complain.

Another thing he said was never to owe anything to anyone if I could help it. So I did not go to work in Fenn Fuller's store, even though he and my father had been good friends at one time. A little later on, when Fenn offered to lend me money to go to college, I didn't care for the sense of obligation, or I might say the debt of gratitude, inherent in the offer, so I declined. Ever since then, every job I took seemed to confirm Fenn Fuller's opinion that I could have done better.

"What's the fella's name?" asked Redington the butcher.

"Dunbar," said Lon Buckley. "He came in here yesterday, and I met him."

Fenn gave the faintest nod, as if to say he had already been told that.

Buckley continued. "Said he came by way of the Rim."

"If he came down that way," said Redington, "he wouldn't have been too far from the project. He could have gotten work there."

"He said he favored ranch work. So I suggested he try the Little Six."

"Work's work," said Fenn. He scratched his whiskers down by his jaw. "As far as that's concerned, Grey would rather do ranch work, too."

I shrugged. It was true enough. I had worked for Tut Whipple building the reservoir here in town, but I hadn't stayed. I handled most of the rocks that lined the spillway and the base of the dam, the rocks I saw each time I rode past. I also helped line the base on the inside, where I now imagined the rocks were settled in ooze and muck. I helped build the lower half of the dam, and I had a hand in putting in the headgate with its posts and beams and three-inch planks. Then I got fed up with Whipple's foreman Stiver, and it being late spring, I went to work for the Little Six roundup. Whipple finished the dam not long after that, and the pond filled up during the next three months as he moved on to work on the larger reservoir.

Redington cleared his throat. "Can't speak for the work itself, but that project's a good deal. It's already brought money into this town, and there's no tellin' what might come of it."

Fenn Fuller stretched his chin forward. "Like I said. Plain as the . . . palm of your hand." He turned his hand over and looked at it.

Redington, who had a bulbous nose with purple shading on the sides of the nostrils, seemed to ignore the comparison. He took a drink of beer and said, "I wonder how far along they are. I've heard they've got a whole camp out there."

"I haven't seen it," said Fenn. "Have you, Grey?"

"Not yet."

Lon Buckley spoke as his eyes kept roving over his saloon. "Well, it's a hell of a lot bigger job than this thing they did here. They've got a lot of dirt to move and a big ditch to dig. Takes a full crew of men."

"I guess he's got some Mexicans workin' there," said Redington.

"They're all right," said Lon. "They'll move the dirt. I heard they had a cook that weighed three hundred pounds. White man."

"He didn't last." Redington took another drink of beer.

"You hear this from your man Mora?" asked Fenn.

The butcher wagged his head. "From various people."

"Oh. Mora's still working for you, though, isn't he?"

"Sure. He still mopes around, though."

Fenn and Buckley nodded.

An uneasy feeling crept into me as it did whenever the subject of Annie Mora came up—or, rather, whenever it was glossed over. She had disappeared not long before I went to work at the Little Six, and all the time I was working on roundup, I wondered if there was any news of her. Then when I got to coming to town on a regular basis, it seemed as if all news was old and no one cared to talk about it. I didn't like that. I thought she deserved more than a brush-off.

Stepping out of my usual role of the boy who did not speak until spoken to, I asked, "Has anyone made an effort to find out what happened to the girl? That is, anyone but her father?"

Fenn Fuller gave me his condescending smile as he said, "We don't really know whether she was abducted or whether she just ran off, Grey."

"I doubt that she ran off."

He gave a small shrug. "It's hard to know until you've got some kind of evidence. Chances are that she'll come back to town some day, plump as a gourd, with two or three kids in tow."

"Keeps her father worried," said Redington.

"Of course," said Fenn. "He's her father. But you know how these old Spanish fathers are. Jealous of their daughters, won't let 'em see anyone, and when they get old enough, they go out the window one night."

I didn't think Annie Mora was the type to go out the window, although maybe she was old enough. She was about seventeen years old when she disappeared. As I recalled her, she was quiet and reserved. She had long, dark hair and a shapely figure, but she didn't make a show of herself. She wore full-length dresses, dark socks, and a shawl or *rebozo* in cold weather.

Fenn Fuller took out his watch and opened it. "Huh. You'd think Henry would've been here by now."

"Oh, he'll come along," said Lon.

They were talking about Henry Dornick, the stone mason. I had had a sense all along that he was absent, but he often came in a little later than the others. The absence that seemed more important to me was Annie Mora's, but when Fenn closed his watch and put it away, I knew the men at the table wouldn't come around to that topic again today.

At the edge of town I stopped at Whipple's place to see Ruth. Before I went to work on the reservoir nearby, I used to do odd jobs for Tut Whipple's wife, and she was always so kind to me that I continued to drop by when I was working for Tut. He and I did not have hard feelings when I quit him and went to work at the Little Six, so I kept my old habit of dropping by from time to time.

On this day she appeared at the door when my horse's hooves sounded in the yard. Her blond, wavy hair hung loose to her shoulders, and she looked fresh and pleasant in a pale blue dress. I dismounted and led my horse forward, and when she smiled, it gave me a light, happy feeling.

"Good afternoon, Grey," she called out. "It's good to see you."

"Nice to see you, too. I was just riding by, and I thought I'd stop in."

"I'm glad you did." She smiled again, not a wide-open smile but enough to show her white, even teeth.

I came to a stop and held the reins loose. "Any news?"

"Not really." Her shiny blue eyes moved over me. "And you, are they treating you well out at the ranch?"

"Just fine."

"For a while you looked as if you'd lost weight, and I thought they weren't feeding you well."

"Oh, we work long days during roundup, but I never go hungry."

She smiled, this time with her mouth closed. "That's good."

"Things are kind of easy right now. Hig sends me into town every few days. No big rush about anything."

"It's good to relax when you can."

I knew she worried about my habits, so I said, "Yeah, I dropped into the saloon for a short visit. Didn't stay long."

"That's just as well." Then her face tensed, and she said, "What's the matter?"

"Oh, nothing."

"There's something, Grey. I can always read your face."

"Nah."

"Did something happen there—something you heard? Oh, I'm sorry. I shouldn't ask."

That was like Ruth, apologizing for something that wasn't her fault, like she did whenever Tut didn't show up on time or when he didn't pay me when he said he would.

"No," I said. "There wasn't anything deep or dark or dangerous."

Though her face relaxed, the worry did not vanish. "But there was something."

I couldn't lie to her or even hold back part of the truth when she asked. She wasn't old enough to be my mother—about twelve years older, as I figured it—but to a boy who lost his mother early in life, a woman who was gentle and took an interest in him was a precious mystery. I loved Ruth, not as a mother and not as a sweetheart, but in some way in between. So I told her what she asked.

"It's about Annie Mora."

"The girl who disappeared."

"That's right."

"You liked her, didn't you, Grey?"

I looked down at my reins as I drew them through my hand. Then I looked up and said, "I think I admired her. From a distance, you know."

"But you miss her?"

I took in a slow breath. "It's not quite that. What's got me bothered is how everyone treats it—her disappearance, I mean."

"Oh, I see. The men in the saloon."

I winced. "Oh, they didn't say anything coarse. It's just that . . . well, nobody seems to care."

Ruth's face was tensed again. "I'm sorry."

"It's not anything you did. But I just don't think it's right that no one cares to look into it. We've got these city fathers—sort of a council, as they imagine themselves—who act as if they're always on the lookout for the good of the town. If someone's got a vicious dog, or a dead cow that's too close for comfort, why, one or two of them will go have a word with the owner. But something like this, they act as if it didn't happen."

"Well, it's hard to get someone else to do things, especially someone who's used to telling others what to do." She smiled, showing a hint of her teeth.

"I know, and there's no point in complaining to you about it. That's not what I dropped by for." I glanced around. "Is there any little thing you need done?"

"Always the good boy. Is that the only reason you ever stop in?"

"No, but it's a good one."

She laughed. "Sometimes I feel guilty, giving you these disagreeable tasks to do."

"If I didn't want to do them, I wouldn't offer."

"I know. And if I didn't save them for you, you'd never come by this way. Just leave me to dry up and blow away like a weed." Her eyes sparkled. "So I'll confess. There's something that's been bothering me, and I saved it for you."

I tied my horse at the rail and followed her around the house. The only thing that separated her backyard from the prairie, except for the outhouse, was a midden heap of bottles, cans, twists of wire, and old boots. A fringe of weeds had grown up around the pile, and now that we were into the latter part of the summer, the weeds had turned pale and gone to seed.

"It's that," she said. "I should have pulled those weeds when they were smaller and the ground was softer."

I raised my eyebrows. "Well, you see, they don't dry up and blow away by themselves."

She laughed like before. "I didn't even think of that. But some do. Tumbleweeds, of course."

"That's true." I glanced around until I located the shovel by the back door. "I don't think it will take me long," I said. "But all the same, you don't need to stand out in the sun." Sometimes, when the weather was fair, she stood around and chatted while I worked, but this day was hot, and she wasn't wearing a sunbonnet.

She shaded her eyes with her hand. "Maybe I can do penance that way."

"Get dirty for nothing," I said, "as well as overheated. I imagine I'll raise a lot of dust and debris."

"Well, in that case I'll find something to do inside."

While she went into the house, I fetched the shovel, which stood next to an old grindstone left by the previous tenant. I pulled down my hatbrim against the sun and went about cutting weeds.

I had finished and was saying good-bye to Ruth in the front yard when Tut Whipple came riding from the direction of town. He waved and brought the horse on in, stopping at my left where I held my horse by the reins.

"Afternoon, Grey."

"Hello, Tut. How's everything?"

"Fine, fine." He glanced at his wife. "Anyone been by?"

"Just Grey."

"I was lookin' to hear from Marston, but no matter." He pushed his hat back on his head.

Tut was a tall, blocky man with a shock of blond hair and a full, straw-colored mustache. He had a full nose like you would see on an Irishmen, but I don't know that he was Irish. I took him for a typical go-ahead American—eager for profit, impatient to get things done, not always concerned about little people or little details.

"Grey was cutting weeds for me," said his wife.

"That's good."

Tut seemed unbothered by my presence. He treated me like a harmless kid, and I think he even saw that I had some use—not just as an errand boy but as a sheepdog as well.

"I should probably be moving along," I said.

"Everything all right out at the ranch?"

"Oh, sure." I never knew him to care about ranches and cattle, but as a man of business he gave a nod to someone else's. I responded in kind. "Things going well on the project?"

"Yeah, yeah. One thing after another, but it's fine."

At that moment, horse hooves sounded on the trail that led into town from the south, along the west end of the pond, and passed by Whipple's house. A dark rider came up the slope and into view, and I saw that it was Dunbar on his buckskin horse. He slowed from a lope to a fast walk and rode by with a toss of the head and a wave of his gloved hand.

Tut Whipple's eyes followed the rider, and a look of displeasure crossed his face. I couldn't define the expression I saw there. It was as if Tut knew the man without having ever seen him before and had an instinctive dislike for him.

"I wonder who that fella is."

"Name's Dunbar. Just hired on at the Little Six."

"Well, I don't like his looks. I wonder what he's doin', ridin' by this way." Tut pulled his hat forward and narrowed his eyes. The blond mustache moved up and down, and I could tell he was clenching his teeth.

"I don't know," I said. "Maybe he came to mail a letter to his mother."

Chapter Two

As we sat at the supper table that evening, Dunbar did not mention having seen me on his way into town. He did not have an air of secrecy about him, however, and I felt I could have mentioned seeing him, but I didn't care to. If he was up to anything, it wasn't my affair, and my father had taught me well enough not to ask personal questions or to make comments that amounted to the same.

Manfred started a platter of fried potatoes down the table. "Help yourselves," he said. "I've got more."

Hig scraped off a serving for himself and handed the platter to Dunbar, who served himself and passed the grub across to me. Manfred brought a second plate for Rumsey and Odell, who sat at the two places on my right. A minute later, a plate of fried beef was coming down the table. When Dunbar had taken a portion and passed the meat over to me, I saw that his dark hair was combed. His mustache moved as he spoke in a harmless tone.

"Well, what about this irrigation project?"

The lines in Hig's face tightened. He swallowed and held silent for a couple of seconds. His right hand rested on the table, and he held his fork upward between his thumb and first finger. "It's a hell of a big waste," he said.

"I thought these projects were supposed to be good for the country," said Dunbar. "Bring water to the land."

Hig glanced at the second plate of beef that Manfred was setting down, and then he answered. "That's what they say. But as far as how much good it does, it depends on who you ask. For a cattleman, the ditch cuts the range in half, makes it harder for cattle to move with the weather. The way this one's laid out, it'll make it damn near impossible for the same man's cattle to graze both sides." Hig turned his squinty brown eyes on Dunbar. "Now what the hell good is that?"

"Doesn't sound like much."

"I'd say. And it's not a new idea they've got. Others have tried it elsewhere, and if you've been around, you know somethin' about it."

Dunbar nodded.

Manfred had brought the coffeepot and got it moving along, and now he took a seat in his usual place at the end of the table. "They do it in the name of opportunity," he said. "Give everyone a fair chance of having a piece of land and making a living off of it. But not many of 'em can make it, so who has the best opportunity? The private speculators that set the whole thing up."

"Private speculators is a nice way of puttin' it," said Higgins. "You could just as well call 'em crooks. Their pals in the Senate let 'em know when the federal government's gonna open up some land, and they buy up twenty or thirty sections at a dollar and a quarter an acre. Then they build the ditch and sell it in three-hundred-and-twenty-acre parcels of irrigated land. Put out leaflets in the cities in the East, and people who have never planted a spud come out thinkin' they'll be tendin' a garden. Them that can't make it, they sell their land back to the speck-you-later, for a hell of a lot less than they paid for it, and they go back to work in a shoe factory."

"Does the land get improved?" asked Dunbar.

Higgins gave a sarcastic laugh. "Imagine these poor would-be dirt farmers, they come out here expectin' to see the Garden of the Lord, because that's what they've been told. They see a miserable piece of cactus and sagebrush, or grassland if they're lucky. In some places, yeah, they turn it into cropland. But you'll see. More often than not, they tear up a piece of pasture land and then leave it to grow weeds. Pah. When I first came here, I didn't know what a tumbleweed was. Now look at 'em. And whenever the dirt gets dug up, the wind carries it away. Hell, what am I tellin' you for? You've seen it."

"Sure."

"So you go back to what Manfred said. Opportunity. And who for? The ones that run the project. You take the man that's behind this one. Ben Marston. He's got friends higher up to help him get in on the federal land, he gets backing from some of the same people who are on the board of his bank, and he lines up just the right kind of man to do the work."

Dunbar made a so-so expression. "I saw the beginnings of that project when I came down from the Rim yesterday."

"And what did you think of it?"

"Like you said about the grangers. They're tearin' up a lot of land. 'Course, if they back up water into that canyon, they'll settle some of the dust."

"Hah. When it comes to rippin' up the country, they're just gittin' started. Wait 'til they dig the ditch."

Dunbar took a bite of meat in his unhurried way. Then he said, "Looks like they've got a full crew out there. How long are they expectin' to take, or does anyone have a figure?"

Manfred spoke again. "No one ever finishes things like that on time anyway, but there's some pressure to get the ditch started pretty soon, while they're still working on the reservoir."

"Do they want it to have it ready in time for next season?"

"That might be part of it, but the fellow in charge is trying to beat the clock in another way. On these private projects, they've got to try to get their money back as soon as they can. On top of that, there are government-funded projects on the way. It'll be a different kind of subsidy, with homesteading along the waterways. All of this is in the works, and it won't come around for two or three years. But when it does, the government can do things on a larger scale—bigger reservoirs, bigger canals, more land—and the government can wait to get its money back. If it ever does."

Dunbar pursed his lips and nodded. "So this fella has got to make hay while the sun shines."

Hig raised his head and looked down at his plate, where he was cutting a chunk of beef. "Some fellas make money in the dark and in the sunshine both."

"Uh-huh," said Dunbar, still in his easy manner. "And I gather that the man who's building the reservoir is the same one who did the pond in town."

Hig sniffed. "That he is."

"Did he do the small one for this same speculator?"

"No, he did that for the town. They got up a fund for it."

"Who uses the water from that?"

"Well, anyone in town who wants to water a horse or a milk cow can do it, of course. And there's water supply in case a building catches on fire. Downstream, a couple of men irrigate hayfields, and some people from town have truck gardens down there, where they raise vegetables and spuds—some of which they sell to the ditch crew."

Dunbar ate a little more, took a drink of coffee, and paused. "You said this ditch-and-dam builder was just the right kind of man."

Hig ran his finger between his neck, which was beginning to wrinkle, and his bandanna, which was creased and compacted from wear. "Yeah. The right kind for the man he's workin' for and the kind of deal it is."

"I guess he's got the experience. Done this work before."

"He's a contractor. Showed he could do the work, at least on a small scale, and now he's got to make good on whatever he said he would deliver on this bigger deal. I really don't know much about him, especially about where he came from or what he did before. I just know he doesn't care about cattle and where they need to find grass and water. Grey there can tell you about him. He worked for him for a while."

Dunbar looked at me with an open expression. "Oh, is that right?"

I was quite sure he had seen me in Whipple's yard earlier that day, but I didn't know if he knew where Whipple lived or what he looked like. "Yes, it is," I answered, "but I don't have much to say, one way or the other. He pushes his men, always in a hurry to get things done. But I didn't know him to beat anyone out of their wages or anything like that."

"Grey knows I don't like the man," said Hig. He laughed and then said, "But we got an agreement. I don't say anything good about Whipple, and Grey don't say anything good about Scriver."

I laughed and said, "Stiver."

"Who's that?" asked Dunbar.

"Tut Whipple's foreman," I answered.

Dunbar nodded.

"That's why I don't have one," said Hig. "In no time at all they think they know more than you do, and they run off good men. You wasn't hopin' to work your way up, now, were you?"

"Oh, no," said Dunbar with a laugh. "I like the way things are."

After supper, Hig rolled one of his thin cigarettes and lit it. He wasn't much over fifty, but he was a tough old cattleman from the old days. He had seen massacres and lynchings, blizzards and droughts and prairie fires. I never saw him smoke on the range, and even around the ranch yard he smoked his cigarette down to a pinch, then watched where he dropped the butt and ground it with his boot heel.

Rumsey and Odell rolled cigarettes and lit them as well. Manfred did not smoke. He set out sardine cans for Hig and the other two. Dunbar pushed his chair back from the table, hiked his right leg up over his knee, and drank from his coffee. All the food was gone, and a lazy silence hung in the air with the cigarette smoke.

Manfred surveyed the table from his seat at the end. He was a serene-looking man, about ten years younger than Higgins but part of the older generation at the Little Six. He had a high forehead with the hairline receding further along his temples. His graying hair covered the tops of his ears and matched the color of his Vandyke beard. He had a narrow face, made to look longer by the beard, and he had a long, narrow nose to match. I do not remember him or anyone else ever calling him anything but Manfred.

As he and Dunbar and I drank coffee and the other three smoked their cigarettes, Manfred seemed to be forming a thought. At length he straightened up, took a breath, and said, "Was there anything you wanted to know about the water project?"

Dunbar raised his eyebrows. "Oh, no. Nothing in particular."

"You seemed interested."

"Just about anything can be interesting," said Dunbar. "When you see change comin' to a country, well, that opens your eyes for a minute. And of course, you wonder if it has anything to do with you. Something like this, I suppose sooner or later we'll cross paths."

"Sure," said Hig. He looked down at the stub of his cigarette. "Even if you boys had the good sense to stay away from that grading crew, the cattle don't."

After a respectful few seconds, Dunbar turned to me and

asked, "Did you work on the stone bridge?"

"No, a mason did that, after I left."

"They must have hauled in a lot of rock."

"Oh, yeah. None of it was there before." As the room went back to silence, I looked down the table at Manfred. "I'll help with the dishes," I said.

Dunbar stood up. "So will I."

Higgins gave a cockeyed glance upward. "Are you that fond of pearl-divin'?"

Dunbar smiled. "Gets your hands clean."

Manfred did not let anyone but himself scrub his cast-iron skillets, so Dunbar and I did the rest. I took the kettle of water that had been heating during supper, and I poured it into the wreck pan. I scattered in some soap flakes and went about washing the cups, then the plates, then the silverware. Dunbar rinsed the items in another pan and placed them on a flour sack spread out on the counter.

The kitchen area occupied the south end of the cook shack, but it was all one big room. As the three of us worked at cleaning up, Rumsey and Odell brought out a deck of cards and got into a game of cribbage. Hig rolled another cigarette and smoked it in silence. None of us in the kitchen spoke, so the only conversation was a bit of talk that went on in the card game. I could feel the presence of Dunbar, Higgins, and Manfred, however, and I imagined each of them was thinking on his own track.

For my part, I was reviewing my impressions of the last couple of days. The exchange of questions and comments during supper made it seem probable that Dunbar was something more than a regular cowpuncher. I thought he might be some kind of a detective. I imagined Higgins and Manfred had hunches similar to mine, but I doubted that any of us had a clear idea of what, if anything, the man was hoping to dig up.

My own understanding of investigators was that they looked for things such as cattle rustlers, labor organizers, and swindlers. My guess was that Dunbar might be looking into crooked deals. I thought Hig might have had the same idea and was hoping Dunbar would find some corruption in the water project and would blow things open. Hig was practical minded. Manfred, on the other hand, was more philosophical, and he might have seen Dunbar's mission as something for a spectator to watch.

I don't know what Hig or Manfred thought, but I did observe that they treated him as part of the fraternity of men who had the common interests of cattle, horses, work, and weather. That was the time-honored way of accepting a stranger who rode for the brand, and it went right along with the way I was raised. So I washed the dishes, passed them to Dunbar, and he rinsed them. Manfred scrubbed his skillets, Hig brooded over his cigarette, Rumsey and Odell moved the pegs on the cribbage board, and harmony prevailed at the Little Six.

On my next trip into town, I rode around the west end of the pond and crossed the plank bridge. Below me, the shallow creek flowed toward the reservoir. I didn't stop until I had ridden up the slope and turned my horse into Whipple's yard.

Ruth came out the front door, shading her eyes with her hand. Her shiny blond hair was wrapped in a bun, and she looked neat and trim in a light gray dress. As I dismounted, she said, "How good of you to come by, and not forget the old lady who lives at the edge of town."

I admired her profile as she stood straight up with her elbow out. "You don't look like you need a cane yet."

She smiled, and her face drew up in the brightness of the day. "Oh, I know. It's just that sometimes I feel old. Beyond my years, as they say."

"You're hardly older than I am."

"Old enough." Her eyes seemed to be looking past me.

I didn't think I had come close to crossing the line, but I didn't want to say or do anything that would spoil our safe comfort, so I retreated. "How's Tut?" I asked.

"Oh, he's fine," came the quick answer. She waved with the hand that had been shading her eyes. "He comes and goes. Sometimes he stays at the camp, you know. Things are always moving too slow for him there, so he leaves in a huff, and then when he's here, he gets impatient to go back out there. You know how he is."

Never happy, I thought. And here he had a lovely wife, wasting away her life at the edge of a dusty town. At some time there must have been something that brought them together, and I could only guess at it. I had gathered, however, that they had not been able to have children, and I sensed it was one more thing for which she held herself at fault. But I was sure that even with children, Tut Whipple would not have been satisfied.

"Oh, things will get better," I said.

"You're so innocent," she said, smiling now but with her head lowered in the sunlight. "I wish I could believe you meant it."

I shrugged and said, "I've got to admit, there's a lot I haven't learned yet."

"Well, I hope there are some things you don't have to learn, but I imagine you'll be saying the same thing to someone else some day."

It was my turn to squint in the bright sun. "Maybe so."

She relaxed and gave a shake of the head. "I shouldn't be filling you so full of pessimism."

"Oh, don't worry," I said. "Hig takes care of that."

She laughed. "We probably give you two different kinds. He'll say you have to hang on and fight until they've cut away the last inch of ground from under your feet, and I'll tell you the best thing to do would be to get on that horse and ride as far away from here as you can."

"I couldn't do that. It's Hig's horse."

"And if you had your own?"

"I could if I wanted."

"But you don't want to."

I shrugged. "I think Hig would tell me that once I got there, things wouldn't be any different than they are here."

"And I would tell you the same thing." Her eyebrows raised. "It hadn't occurred to me that Mr. Higgins and I would have that much in common."

I tipped back my hat and scratched my forehead. "I don't think it would have occurred to me, either."

A wistful look came upon her face. "You know, Grey, when I think of men like that, men who live on those distant ranches, men without women, I think of how different they are from those of us who live in houses in town. But now when I think of the similarities rather than the differences, it seems to make a good deal of sense."

"I think as far as pessimism goes, he's got a long head start on you."

"Maybe he does, but as you're quick to remind me, I'm still young." Now her blue eyes sparkled. "But enough of that. No need to corrupt you younger ones before your time."

"It's not as if I'm still spinning tops and playing marbles."

"Oh, I know. But we shouldn't be rushing you to your disillusionments. You have plenty of time to get there by yourself."

"I hope so."

Now her eyes turned soft, and I thought she was going to reach out and touch me, but she kept her repose as she spoke. "When you're young and free, Grey, it can be the best part of your life. The trouble is, we spend that time poorly, or too quickly, because we don't know how to make the best of it. We don't know what we want, and then the time is past."

"I hope it doesn't happen to me that way."

"See? There I am, being pessimistic again."

"No, that's all right," I said. "You've seen more of life than I have, and I ought to be able to benefit from it." I felt as if we were moving closer together, even though we stood in our places there in the sunlight. "Like the part about not knowing what we want."

"Oh, that. Well, yes, that's the way it seems to go. Then later, people want what they can't have."

"That's not all bad," I said. "A man's reach—"

"Should exceed his grasp," she added, to finish the quotation. "But I'm talking about something else as well."

I nodded. I thought she meant children, but she could have meant other things she had not found in her life with Tut.

She went on. "I don't know what comes next—for example, when one gets to the age of Mr. Higgins, or older. Perhaps I'll let you know, if I get there." She didn't seem to like that prospect, for she gave a quick shake of the head and said, "How about you, Grey? Do you know what you want?"

At that moment, as at other moments when I loved her hopelessly, I wanted her. But I had to say something to cover myself. "I think so. One thing, at least."

Her eyes opened in curiosity. "And what is that?"

"I want to know what happened to Annie Mora."

Now her expression turned coy as she said, "Is that what you want? Are you sweet on her?"

"No, not really. Not any more than I said before."

"Then why do you want to know what happened to her?"

I looked at my boots and then up. "I guess somebody should, especially when so many other people don't seem to care."

In quick response she said, "Well, I do."

"Oh, I didn't mean you," I said, just as quick. "I couldn't find fault with you, you know."

Ruth's eyes softened again. "You're so gallant. You're the only one I know who thinks that way."

We stood there for a moment without speaking. No sound came from the town—not even the rapping of a hammer or the bark of a dog.

"Have you got anything that needs to be done?" I asked.

"Nothing I can think of."

"Well," I said, fidgeting with my reins, "I suppose I should be moving on."

She held me with her sky-blue eyes. "Don't be a stranger," she said. "You never need a reason to stop in and say hello."

"I know."

"And don't pay me any mind if I seem gloomy like I did today."

I tipped my head. "I didn't notice it."

She gave a light laugh. "You *are* getting to be gallant. You're going to be dangerous."

"I don't know when."

The sound of hoofbeats came from the plank bridge, so I waited to see who it was before I mounted up.

As a tan hat came into sight, I thought the rider might be Tut. In another minute I saw his shadowed face, then the sorrel horse with the narrow blaze. Tut did not slow down from a lope when he came onto level ground, and when he turned off the road he stopped the animal in a few yards. Dust rose and followed him as he stepped down from the horse and squared around.

" 'Lo, Grey."

"Good afternoon."

"Gettin' hot," he said.

"Somewhat."

He looked at his wife and said, "Wonder if you could bring us a drink of water."

Her mouth bunched as she nodded and went to the house.

As soon as she was inside, Tut let go of his matter-of-fact manner. He motioned with his head backward, as if toward the range country, and said, "What about this fella you call Dunbar?"

"I don't know. What about him?"

"I wonder what he's up to."

"I don't know if he's up to anything."

"Well, I don't like him."

"Just from what you saw of him when he rode by the other day?"

"Oh, no. I saw him before that. The day he rode down from the Rim, travelin' with his bed horse. Then he's been out lookin' things over once or twice since then."

"Once, or twice?"

"I saw him once. One of the men said he thought he saw him before that."

"Well, I don't know anything."

"Does your boss send him out there to spy on us?"

The question took me by surprise. "I don't think so. Hig sends him out to check cattle, just like the rest of us."

Tut made a small spitting action, as if he was trying to get rid of a fleck of tobacco. "I was just wonderin' if your boss brought him in to spy on us or to put up obstacles."

"What kind?"

"I don't know 'til I see 'em. But I do know that a drifter like that can cause trouble."

I hadn't thought to classify Dunbar as a drifter, and I found it curious that Tut, who moved from place to place with his own work, would choose that way to belittle a man who had two good-looking horses and a full outfit.

"Well, I don't think Hig brought him in," I said. "I'm pretty sure he came on his own."

"Doesn't matter much. His kind isn't gonna bother me."

It seemed apparent to me that Dunbar's presence was bothering Tut already, and in spite of his tossing it off, or maybe because of it, Tut gave me the impression that he had some inkling of what Dunbar might find. I thought it might be a good joke on everybody if Dunbar wasn't looking for anything, but I didn't think the town of Winsome was going to get to enjoy that kind of a jest.

Ruth came out with a pitcher of water and two glasses. Looking at me, she said, "I'm sorry I didn't offer you some earlier."

"It's all right," I answered. She poured until my glass was half-full and I pushed it upward. "I wasn't very thirsty, and you didn't put me to work with a shovel."

"You want to work with a shovel," said Tut, "I've got plenty of that for you."

"I'm all right for the time being."

He gave a smile, which was never very cheery. "Help you work up an honest thirst."

I had heard him say before that men who worked in the saddle just sat on their asses, so I knew what part of his comment to avoid. "Sometimes I save it up," I said.

He drank from the glass his wife handed him. Then still in his way of being witty, he said, "I know. I've seen where you tie your horse. If you worked for me, you wouldn't be hangin' around the saloons nearly so much."

Ruth held the pitcher with both hands. In a pleasant tone she said, "Oh, you don't spend that much time there, do you, Grey?"

I smiled as I handed the empty glass to her. "Hardly at all," I said.

I rode through town without stopping at the Whitepaw Saloon.

I went past it and the livery stable, crossed the wide street that came in from the south, and kept going east. Ringing blows came from the blacksmith shop on my right, and voices came from the work site on my left, where Henry Dornick and his men were building the walls of the bank. Dornick himself was holding a stone mason's hammer and pointing with his free left hand at a window opening. I knew him by his short-brimmed, low-crowned hat, dusty as always. He turned and waved as I rode by.

I waved back. I passed the town well and water trough on my left, then the wagon and buggy shop. On my right, a man leaned on a push broom in the large open doorway of the grain warehouse.

Crossing the next street, I saw nothing of interest in the coal yard. Buildings were farther apart now, with more empty lots than on the street front of the three main blocks in town. I passed a heap of rubble on my right and then turned in to the place I was headed for.

The Castle was a roadhouse-style tavern that, in spite of its name, was made of lumber. It sat on a rock foundation that I don't think Dornick made, as some of the pieces had crumbled loose. It could just as well have been called the Last Chance, as it was the last building on the way out of town going east.

The place did not have its own well. The proprietor's lackey hauled water from the town well every few days, and he dumped it into a cistern out front. The owner kept the tank covered with boards, and either he or his help brought water up with a windlass and bucket. As I tied my horse to the rail, I saw that the board cover had a wet circle on it, where someone must have set a full bucket not long before.

I went inside and stood for a moment, taking in the place as my eyes adjusted from the bright day outside. No one stood at the bar along the left wall. Clark, the proprietor, sat at a table folding a newspaper. He took off his eyeglasses and turned my way.

"What's your pleasure today, young feller?"

"Maybe a little to eat," I said.

"We can do that." He shifted in his chair and called toward the back where the kitchen was located. "Hey, Rachel. Got someone here."

I took a table near the window on the right side of the place. In less than a minute, Rachel came out of the dim background and stood near my table.

"How are you today?" she asked.

"Just fine. How about you?"

"Oh, I'm fine, too."

I took a quick glance at her, and I couldn't agree more. She had long, black hair, deep-colored eyes, and a complexion like dark honey. She had a shapely figure that was not concealed by her full dress, open at the top and showing smooth, lovely skin. I made myself look her in the eyes.

"What do you have in the pot today?" I noticed her red earrings as I heard her answer.

"My mother made a very good stew. I'm sure you'll like it."

"I'm sure of it, too. Maybe some biscuits, or bread?"

"There's some bread."

"That sounds just right."

"Very well." She turned and gave a quarter-whirl, which I flattered myself to think was for my benefit, and went back to the kitchen.

Clark had taken up his glasses and newspaper again. He was a middle-aged man who had put on some weight, and every few minutes he brought up a sound from the bottom of his throat.

Rachel brought me a bowl of stew and a plate with four thick slices of bread. "Something else? A glass of water?"

I preferred not to drink water that came out of the cistern, so

I said, "No, this is fine."

She did not seem in a hurry to leave. "And how is your work?" she asked.

"Oh, it's all right. Not very hard right now." I met her eyes, which had a dark shine to them. "Any news around here?"

"No, not much." Rachel was a couple of years older than Annie Mora and they had been friends of sorts, but she didn't seem to be thinking of Annie at the moment. Or maybe she was and didn't believe that no news was good news.

A couple of seconds later, her mother's voice came from the kitchen. *"¡Raquel!"*

"That's for me," said Rachel. "Enjoy your meal."

"Thanks. I'll see you later."

With a flash of red earring and a swish of the dress as before, she returned to the dim recesses of the Castle.

Chapter Three

Hig sent Dunbar and me on a long ride to the southwest, to push any Little Six cattle back to our part of the basin. Dunbar said he liked to keep his own horses in shape, so instead of riding a ranch horse he brought his blue roan out of the pasture and saddled it. I rode a deep-chested sorrel out of my string, a horse that I knew had the endurance for the day ahead.

We left the ranch when the shadows of morning gave the country a dappled look. The air was brisk enough that Dunbar wore a canvas coat and I had on a denim jacket. We both wore leather riding gloves. We let the horses lope for a couple of miles and then settled into a fast walk.

"Nice country," said Dunbar as we moved along. "Good grass, plenty of room. Not a lot of fences."

"What do you think of it for farm country?"

His gaze went out far ahead as he answered. "Not much, really. I try not to have an opinion on how other men make their living, provided they don't go out of bounds. You see places where they cut down every stick of timber big enough to make a chair leg, and they leave enough slash to burn down the whole country. Or in minin' country, they have heaps of tailings and pools of acid. On and on. Build slaughter houses on the river and dump the guts and manure right into the next town's water supply. But as long as none of it's against the law, it's hard to see where one man's opinion is goin' to do much." He turned to me. "Not that I'm a fatalist, you know. I'm not the kind to say, 'Oh, people are going to do what they want, so I'll just stay out of their way and take what I can get for myself.' "

"So what does a man do—a man alone?"

Dunbar's dark eyes came around. "He does his work. He doesn't have a hand in things he doesn't believe in. That doesn't mean he runs and hides from the rest of the world, though I don't blame prospectors and sheepherders and hermits if that's what they're doin'."

"So in other words, if a man wants to lead a good life, a large part of it is in what he doesn't do."

"That's a way of lookin' at it. Not quite as stern as some of the Ten Commandments, and not quite as gentle as the golden rule. If you want to make your livin' with cattle, you don't change brands, you don't forge bills of sale, and so forth. And if you're a farmer, you don't steal water, and you don't take payment on grain you don't deliver."

"So that's all a fella has to do."

Dunbar wagged his eyebrows. "Oh, probably not. The cattleman shouldn't get together with other cattlemen for the purpose of hirin' paid killers to trim down the opposition. Your farmer shouldn't get together with other farmers to bribe a senator to get a government subsidy for a reservoir or a rail line."

"Do you think someone's doing that?"

"Huh," he said. "Just about any bad thing that people can do is bein' done all the time. Here we are, you and me, ridin' across God's golden earth without a care in the world, tradin' cow country philosophy, and elsewhere in the country at large, people are stabbin' one another, bludgeoning, strangling, torturing, looking into the eyes of their victims and gloating—" He broke off and took a breath. "So I'd guess that somewhere, someone is bribin' a senator." After a second he added, "Sorry if I ventured too far there."

"Not at all," I said. "Ideas are ideas."

"Sometimes that's all they are, though we try not to just get by on talk."

I glanced at the Rim in the distance, where white and tan bluffs were interspersed with dark canyons of shadow and cedar. "Let me go back to an earlier idea," I said.

"Go ahead."

"If a good part of what a man does is a matter of looking out for what he shouldn't do, what else is there?"

"He does his work."

"All right. We already covered that. But what else does a man do? If he doesn't fight the bigger things, does he look the other way?"

Dunbar pushed his mouth forward in a thoughtful pose. "If by the bigger things, you mean timber and minin' and such, I'd say it's not a fight a man can win by himself. I don't know of anyone who ever went up against the railroad and won. But man to man, sometimes you can do somethin'. Keep someone from doin' wrong, or bring 'em to account for somethin' they did."

"Like the stabbing and bludgeoning. Just for examples."

"Something like that."

"So a man alone can do something."

He shrugged. "Some can. Not everyone wants to. All of this is still just cow country philosophy, of course. You and me, under Heaven's dome."

"Of course."

"Your father could have told you some of this, or maybe he did. He was a lawyer, wasn't he?"

"Yes, he was. You aren't, though, are you?"

"Oh, hell, no. I'm a cowpuncher."

Whatever else Dunbar might have been, I saw soon enough that he knew his way around horses and cattle. Each time we brought cattle out of one of the canyons along Decker Rim, he cut out the Little Six stock and gave it to me to push out onto the plain.

At midday we took a rest where a spring trickled out of the shade in one of the canyons. Manfred had sent along some biscuits and rather hard cheese in a linen bag, which I took out of my saddlebag. Dunbar said he wanted to wash his hands and face, so I held his reins. He set his hat upside-down on a slab of sandstone and laid his gloves inside the crown. Before he knelt at the spring, he glanced around the rim of the canyon. Then he crouched, cupped his hands, and caught water to splash on his face.

When he was done, he stood bareheaded with his shoulders squared and his hands turned out to the sun. At that moment I noticed something I hadn't seen before. It looked as if he had been burned in the palm of his right hand. Something stirred in the bottom of my mind, but I didn't place it, and then the moment was past. Dunbar put on his hat, tucked his gloves in his belt, and took both sets of reins from me. It was my turn to kneel where the cool water flowed out of the heart of the earth.

As we ate our lunch, I remarked that the projected canal would cut off this part of the range from the Little Six cattle.

"They'll be able to cross it in the wintertime," he said.

I recalled seeing some of these canyons in the winter, when snow clung to the ledges and piled deep in the draws. "That's the worst time of year for them to get caught in some of these places," I said.

"Oh, yeah," he answered. "I didn't mean there was much good to it."

I gazed out at the grass and sagebrush. "Do you think they'll be able to bring the ditch this far in a season?"

He shrugged. "Depends on how many men and how much equipment what's-his-name can bring in."

"You mean Whipple?"

"Yeah, him."

I didn't think I was breaking a confidence when I said, "He seems to be worried that someone's going to put up obstacles."

"Oh, it could happen. But like as not, he'll put up obstacles himself."

"You seem to know him."

"Not in person. Not yet." Dunbar glanced around the canyon, where dark trees and bushes grew down the slopes and into the fold of the drainage. "You know what I think?"

"What?"

"I think these chokecherries are just about ripe."

I could see the dark, pea-sized fruit from where I sat. "Don't tell Manfred," I said. "He'll have us all out here with tin pails."

"What's wrong with that?" asked Dunbar with a smile. "All work's good work."

"I know," I said. "Toiling in the garden of the Lord."

"Don't worry," said Dunbar. "I won't say a word. But if he likes to make chokecherry jelly, he knows when they ripen."

A couple of days later, Higgins told the four of us riders to get the tools together to go cut corral posts and rails. Dunbar and I had seen some good cedars and young cottonwoods along the Rim, so we had an idea of where to go.

As Rumsey and Odell were hitching the horses to the wagon, Hig came out of the bunkhouse and watched for a couple of minutes. Then he said, "Three of you ride, and one of you drive the wagon. Manfred's going along, too. He says it's time to pick a few chokecherries. You boys get him a few bucketfuls while you're at it."

I could tell no one wanted to go in the wagon, as each of us saddled up without saying anything to the others. At about the time we were done, Manfred put a washtub and four tin pails in the wagon to go along with the axes and crosscut saws. Then he came out again with a rifle in a leather case. When he had laid it under the seat, he asked, "Who's going to ride with me?"

"I will," said Dunbar. He led the blue roan to the rear of the wagon to tie it.

"That's fine," said Manfred as he looked around at the rest of us. "You three, each of you take one of these pails and go ahead. You ought to have them full by the time we get there."

Rumsey and Odell glanced at each other and then at Dunbar. It gave me a moment's amusement to see Rumsey in his engraved leather wrist cuffs and Odell in his calfskin vest, each taking the pail that Manfred handed out. Then I took mine, and the three of us mounted up and took off.

It takes a good while to pick enough chokecherries to cover the bottom of a bucket, and a lot longer to fill one up, so we were just getting started with the wood cutting when Manfred called us in for lunch. He had a layout of sliced bread and cold beef on the tailgate, plus a cream can of water and five tin cups.

Manfred sat on the tailgate while the rest of us sat on the ground cross-legged and put away the lunch. At about the time we were finishing, Rumsey spoke up.

"Say, Manfred. What would you think of loanin' us your rifle?"

The cook's face seemed to lengthen as he raised his eyebrows. "What for?"

"There's a coyote over there, slinkin' its way up the canyon. Like to take a shot at it."

"Just a waste of shells."

"Ah, come on. We picked your cherries for you, didn't we?"

"Well, I suppose you did. Go ahead, but leave me two shells in case I see a deer."

Rumsey pushed himself up and moved around the off side of the wagon. Odell got up and followed him. Manfred eased off the tailgate and stood on the ground.

Rumsey pulled out the rifle, levered in a shell, and settled into position across the front of the wagon. A second later, the crash of the gunfire made me flinch.

"Missed him," said Rumsey as the lever action went clickety-click. The next shot split the air like the first one did, and I could hear the reverberation in the canyon.

"Missed him again," said Odell. "Let me try."

"Nah, he's gone."

Rumsey put the gun in its case, and the two of them came back to the tailgate. Manfred poured water into the cups and handed them out. Dunbar and I were still sitting on the ground, and no one said anything for a couple of minutes.

As I was about to get up, the sound of horse hooves came from the north. I went ahead and stood up, and Dunbar did the same. At that moment a rider came around the toe of the bluff that jutted out from the canyon.

I recognized the horse and rider together. The horse was a yellowish-white plug that belonged to Tut Whipple, and the man aboard was his foreman, Mick Stiver. Even without the horse I would have known him a mile away for the billed cloth cap he wore, puffed up around the top like a railroad engineer's. As usual he wore a dull white work shirt, brown suspenders, a gray-and-white striped vest, and matching pants. He had his head cocked, as he did half the time, and he rode toward our wagon with his free hand hovering near his pistol butt.

Rumsey and Odell had squared around to meet him. "What do you want?" called out Odell, not in the friendliest of tones.

"Came to see what the shootin' was about."

"What's it to you?"

Stiver rode forward, stopped the white horse, and slid off. "I've got men workin' back there," he said.

"Oh, piss," said Odell. "They've got to be four, five miles off."

"Our right-of-way goes all along here," said Stiver. "In fact, your wagon horses are standin' on it."

"Put up a fence." Odell was shorter than average, with a light build, and he had blond hair with a sparse mustache, but he gave a hard look. He had a pistol on his hip just as Stiver did, and I had seen him a hundred times brush his hand across the grip. At the moment, he stood with his feet planted, his hand dangling, and his light brown eyes fixed on Stiver.

"You'll see who ought to put up a fence," came the answer.

"Go blow your horn," said Odell, his mouth barely moving. "You know the law in this state. You fence animals out, not in. You want to keep stock off your land, if it's yours, you fence 'em out."

Stiver's blue eyes had a glint to them, and his tawny mustache moved as he spoke. "Don't get too smart with me."

"What if I do?"

Rumsey's voice came up. "Take it easy, Tim. He just came to see what the noise was."

"Oh, the hell he did. He came all this way just to snoop on us."

"Well, forget it."

"Listen to your pal," said Stiver. "And as for snoopin', I don't have to. I've got free run of this right-of-way."

"Just see that you stay on it."

Stiver had already turned toward his horse. He looked over his shoulder and said, "Put up a fence." He grabbed the saddle horn with his left hand and the cantle with his right. He poked his foot in the stirrup, pulled himself up, and swung his right hand around to the pommel.

I've never liked that way of getting onto a horse, and it always gave me satisfaction to see him do it that way.

As the white horse trotted away, I heard Dunbar's voice at my side.

"Who's that pleasant fellow?"

"Mick Stiver. Foreman for Tut Whipple."

"The one you have the agreement about."

I shook my head, then caught his meaning. "Oh, yeah. With Hig."

Odell came back to the tailgate and took a drink of water from his cup. When he finished he took off his hat, a light-colored thing with a rolled brim, and dragged his cuff across his forehead. Then he put on his hat and took the leather gloves from his vest pocket. I thought he was calming down until he slapped the gloves across his forearm and said, "Come here to snoop, that's what."

Rumsey spoke again. "Oh, forget it, Tim. It's nothin' to get hurt over."

"If I had a monkey, I wouldn't let him wear a hat like that."

Rumsey smiled. "Well, that's just the difference between you and Tut Whipple."

We worked at gathering posts, poles, and firewood for a couple of days. We saw no more of Stiver or any of that crew, and everything went back to normal at the ranch. Higgins set us to peeling corral poles, and when we were done with that, he said it was time for me to go to town again. Dunbar asked if he could go along, and Hig said it would be all right.

I saddled a dark horse, and Dunbar saddled his buckskin. We rode out of the ranch yard after noon dinner, with the sun overhead and a dry breeze out of the northwest. My horse had a smooth gait under me, and I enjoyed the sun's warmth as it reflected off the horse and the saddle. Dunbar was not talkative today, which was all right with me. I didn't care for the company, as I preferred to be on my own when I went to town, but since we were both on the job I couldn't complain. I just kept to myself. Dunbar, meanwhile, had his unknowing, unbothered air about him.

When we came out of the hills at the edge of town, he asked me what I usually did on these trips in addition to picking up the mail. Without thinking very much, I said I sometimes checked in on Ruth Whipple.

"Is that the wife of this fella that does the ditch work?" he asked.

"Yes," I said. I found his innocence irritating. I was sure he already knew the answer, just as I was sure he knew who Stiver was when he asked.

"Huh," he said by way of answer.

"Sometimes I drop by on the way in, and sometimes I wait 'til I'm on my way home."

"We could go that way now," he said. "I wouldn't stay. Just long enough to see who she is."

Now I was irritated even more, as I was sure he had seen the three of us standing in the yard that day. But I figured it was the best way of getting rid of him, so I agreed.

We rode around the west end of the pond, across the plank bridge, and up the slope.

"Whoa," said Dunbar, bringing the buckskin to a stop.

I drew up also and followed his line of sight to the southeast. I saw nothing but the blue surface of the pond, shining in the afternoon sun.

"Pretty," he said. "You-all did a good job."

I had no sense of how sincere he was, and I wanted to move him along. "I didn't do all that much," I said.

He turned, and the unguarded expression on his face gave me an odd feeling. Then he regained his light manner and said, "He lives over there, doesn't he?"

"That's right." I touched my heel to the dark horse and set off at a trot.

Ruth did not come out until the two of us had stopped in the yard and dismounted. When she did come out, she was wearing a light blue sunbonnet that matched the color of her dress. Her voice sounded cheerful as she said, "Well, hello, Grey."

"Good afternoon, Ruth. We were on the way into town, so we stopped to say hello."

She gave me what seemed like a perfunctory smile and said, "I'm glad you did." Then she glanced at Dunbar and back at me.

"This is Dunbar," I said, not knowing a first name for him and not being alert enough to think of saying "mister."

She nodded.

"Works with us at the ranch."

Dunbar took off his hat, and his dark hair was glossy in the sun as he tipped his head forward. "Honored to meet you, ma'am."

Her face drew up as she made a half-smile. "And the same here."

I could tell she was uncomfortable, so I tried a light tone when I said, "Had any trouble with rats?"

"Why, no," she said. "Have you?"

"Not much. Just thought I'd ask."

"Oh, I see. Being thoughtful." She looked at Dunbar, who still held his hat in front of him. "Don't you find him that way, Mr. Dunbar?"

"All the time."

No one spoke for a moment, and then Dunbar said, "Well, I think I'll be on my way."

"Very well," said Ruth. "So nice to meet you."

"Thank you, and likewise."

He swung aboard the buckskin and rode toward town. She watched him until he was fifty yards away, and then she spoke to me in a sharp whisper.

"Why did you bring him here? You know it could be trouble."

"I'm sorry," I said. "It wasn't my idea. He said he wouldn't stay long."

"Well, thank goodness he didn't." Her voice relaxed. "And you and your rats."

"I felt like I should say something."

"I hadn't even thought of it, but you know, I haven't seen a rat since we moved here. Mice maybe, but not a rat."

"They're not a big item like they are in some places, but they're around. Keep down the weeds and rubbish around the house, and that helps."

She had a vacant expression for a moment and then said, "Oh, yes."

"Anyway," I went on, "if there's anything you'd like me to do, I could spare a few minutes."

A soft smile came onto her face. "What a sweet boy. As it so happens, I do have something. I got a delivery of stove wood the other day, and some of the pieces are too long. I sorted them out." She had lowered her head, and I could see her eyelashes and the ridge of her bonnet as she gave a coy imitation of being shy.

"Give me the ax," I said.

The pieces were not thick, none of them bigger around than my wrist, so I went at them pretty well. Sometimes on the last stroke, one of the halves would flip and fly end over end across the back yard, so I had some picking up to do. As I was finishing, I heard Tut's voice behind me.

"I see she put you to work."

"Oh, it's not much," I said.

He held his head up as he looked down at the pieces of firewood. "They should cut it the right length to begin with."

I put the last couple of pieces on the pile and set the ax by the grindstone. It occurred to me, as in the past, that he did not apologize or even say a word of thanks for someone doing chores that should be his. When I turned to face him, he spoke.

"I saw that fellow Dunbar when I came through town."

"I believe he's here."

"Must not be much to do out there at the ranch, I guess."

"Oh, we've been busy. You know, Hig sends me in here once in a while." I saw a piece of firewood that escaped me earlier, so I went to pick it up.

"Does it take two to carry the mail?"

"Not what little we get." I straightened up. "I think there was something he wanted to buy."

"Oh?"

"Rat poison, or something like that."

"I imagine. Got nothin' better to do. I tell you, I'd like to have this fellow workin' for me. He'd see how the honest sweat runs."

"I don't think Dunbar digs ditches."

"He probably doesn't do much of anything."

I was struck by how forced, how imperfect, the man's contempt was, but I thought I had roiled him enough. "Is Ruth in the house?" I asked.

"Sure. Do you need something?"

"I could use a drink of water."

That seemed to please him. "I'll tell her to bring you one," he said.

On my way through town, I saw that Dornick's crew had made progress on the walls of the bank. One worker was scraping off the platform where the men mixed the mortar, and a couple of wheelbarrows sat nearby. Dornick in his dusty clothes was directing two workers who were setting up a scaffold. He had his pipe in his hand, and he waved at me as I went by.

I had not seen Dunbar's horse when I came through the middle of town, and I had no idea of whether he had gone back to the ranch. I told myself that I did not have to answer to him, and I was glad not to see his buckskin in front of the Castle.

I tied my horse at the rail, noticed the dry boards covering the cistern, and went inside. A man I didn't know stood at the bar, and Clark stood on the other side, talking in a matter-of-fact tone. I was the only other person in sight, so I walked to the table near the window and took a seat.

From behind the bar, Clark pulled on a string that hung from a metal eye hook on the ceiling. I heard the faint tinkle of a bell in the kitchen, and a few seconds later I saw the door swing open. Rachel came out and made her way to my table.

It looked as if she was wearing the same dress as before, but her earrings were of a deep blue stone. It did me good to look at her and to return her smile.

"Good afternoon," she said. "Would you like something to eat?"

"Just a little something. I'm not very hungry. You don't have any cake or pie, do you?" I looked up at her and met her dark eyes.

"No, but there are some biscuits and jam."

"That would be good. With a cup of coffee if you have it."

She smiled as she tipped her head to the side. "I think we have some."

I watched her go back to the dusky area of the kitchen. A minute later, she came into view again and brought me my order.

"Thank you," I said as she set it down.

"You're welcome." She straightened up and stood back half a step but did not move away.

"How have you been?" I asked. "It seems like a while since I've seen you."

"Oh, I've been fine. And you?"

"Well enough. Glad to see you. Wish I could come by more often."

She had her hands together and gave a faint smile. "I'm almost always here. I don't go anywhere."

"Neither do I, really."

"Everything's so far away."

"It sure is." I peeked at the crockery jam pot, but I didn't want to start eating because I didn't want to send her away. "What's new in town?" I asked.

"Oh, nothing, I don't think."

"Same here."

"Well, maybe one thing," she said.

"Oh, what's that?"

Her eyes met mine for a second and moved away. "One of the neighbors had a baby."

"That's good." Talk of babies did not register very deep with me at that point.

"They're going to have a baptism on Sunday."

"Oh, that's good, too." I glanced at the jam again and thought of the chokecherries we had picked. I wondered if she liked chokecherry jelly.

"They're going to have a little *fiesta,* you know."

"Oh." My interest picked up.

"Just a little thing. Some food, and maybe a cake." She gave a shrug.

Our eyes met again. "Sounds nice," I said.

"It should be. You know, I mention it because you said before that you'd like to go to a Mexican party."

"Sure, I would."

"Well, it's on Sunday. You could come if you want. If you have time."

"I'm sure I will. What time of day?"

"Put it at, let's say, one o'clock."

"Over at, um . . ." I didn't want to come right out and say what the white people called those few blocks.

She said it for me. "Mexican town. *La colonia.*"

What little tension I had felt now vanished. I took a full look at her. "I'll be there. Anything I can bring?"

She smiled, and her eyes sparkled. "Oh, a couple dozen tamales. No, if you just bring yourself, that will be enough."

"I'll do that."

"Very well," she said. "We'll see you then." As she turned to leave, her mother's voice called her name in Spanish. She looked over her shoulder and gave me one last smile as she walked to the kitchen.

Chapter Four

On Sunday after breakfast, the four of us hands had gone back to the bunkhouse and were lounging around. Rumsey had rolled a smoke in his easygoing way and was taking casual puffs as he lay on his bunk. Odell was sitting at the table, rubbing and oiling his six-gun with a smudged scrap from an undershirt. Dunbar sat on the edge of his bunk cleaning his fingernails. I sat on a chair near the door, where I could hear a meadowlark out on the prairie.

After a while I stood up and said, "I left a kettle of water heating on the stove, and I'm going to go get it so some of us can shave." Rumsey and Dunbar said "Fine" and "All right." Odell was lighting a cigarette he had just rolled, and he seemed intent on that bit of work.

I went across the dogtrot and into the cook shack, where I used a dishcloth to pick up the kettle by its thick wire handle. I took it to the bunkhouse, where I poured about half a gallon into an enamel basin. Dunbar set out the other basin and poured water for himself.

From the sideboard I took the crockery cup where I kept my shaving soap and brush, and I daubed in some hot water. As I worked up a lather, I saw that Dunbar was doing the same. I finished shaving a little ahead of him, as he took some care to trim his large dark mustache. I carried my basin to the back door and pitched the water.

Rumsey had gotten up and tested the remaining water in the

kettle. "I can use this," he said.

I dipped a couple of handfuls to rinse the basin and then gave it to him. At about that time, Dunbar finished shaving and pitched his water.

"Did you want to shave, Tim?" he asked.

"Not yit," said Odell. He had finished with his six-gun and was oiling his rawhide lariat, which was an item of pride with him.

I went to my bunk, pulled out my bag from underneath, and took out a pair of clean socks. I set them on the bunk and began to unfold a clean shirt I had left on my pillow earlier.

"What time are you leaving?" asked Dunbar.

"In a little while, I'd say. Why?"

"Well, I guess you're goin' to the Mexican party, too. I s'pose we can ride together."

I was going, too. I should say so. As far as I saw it, he was the newcomer. But at least he wasn't inviting himself along with me this time.

When we got out onto the trail, I asked him how he came about getting invited to this little fiesta.

"Oh, I was just talkin' to one of the men, and he mentioned it. Said I was welcome to come. Always good people for a party, you know, and I like a chance to practice my Spanish."

He didn't ask me how I got invited, but I imagined whoever invited him also knew I was going and told him so. I wondered why he was playing so close to the chest about not saying who "mentioned it" to him, as I would figure it out soon enough anyway.

We rode into town by way of Whipple's place but did not stop. Dunbar did not even give the house a glance. We rode on, across the main street and past a church, then a couple of blocks more until we came to what Rachel called *la colonia.* It began on the north end of a block. The south half was empty and littered, and along the alley, crossways, a motley fence marked the back yards of a handful of houses facing north. Across the street from those houses sat a dusty little plaza with straggling shrubs and a couple of spindly elms about four feet tall. Houses lined the east and west sides of this plaza, and a lone house sat at the north end. In the middle sat an open shelter, a roof on poles, where about a dozen people had already gathered and were sitting in chairs.

By the time we had our horses tied and our cinches loosened, a man came out from the shelter and greeted Dunbar. I recognized him as Mr. Mora, Annie's father, who worked for Redington the butcher. He shook Dunbar's hand and exchanged some words in Spanish. Then he motioned to me and said, "Come on."

"Momento," said Dunbar. He went to his saddle bag and took out a package wrapped in brown paper.

When we got to the shade, Dunbar handed the package to one of the women and said something. Within a minute, several children gathered around, and as the woman opened the package, I saw that Dunbar had brought candy.

More people arrived, among them a couple of men who worked on Whipple's crew. They nodded to me and took seats among the other men. Dunbar sat with the group of men, chatting in Spanish.

I sat at the edge of the group, not quite with the men and not with the women. I felt somewhat like an outsider, but not because of the way I was treated. People nodded to me and smiled. Voices rose and fell in cadence around me, and children ran through laughing. I wondered what the food would be like, whether the cake would be sweet, and when Rachel was going to show up.

Then she appeared, walking through the group of women and saying *"Buenas tardes"* as she gave her hand or laid it upon a shoulder. When she made her way to me, she smiled and said, "Good afternoon. I see you came with your friend."

I stood up and took off my hat. "We work together," I said.

"That's good. They say he knows the Mexican people."

"It looks as if he does."

"And you? Did you come to lose your money at cards, or lose your horse in a race?"

I opened my eyes wide. "I don't think so."

"Don't worry," she said, laughing. "I'm only teasing. This is a baptism, not the *fiesta de San Felipe.*"

"I don't see the baby."

"He's still inside. Actually, they baptized him this morning. This is just the dinner." She motioned with her hand. "Sit down. We're going to bring the food out pretty soon."

Two men set up a long table with benches and planks, and then a procession of women brought out clay dishes and iron pots full of food. There was lamb in red chile sauce, deep-fried cubes of pork, rice, beans, a dish of cooked green chiles and white cheese, and stacks of corn tortillas wrapped in towels.

The women served up the food, and they tended to the men first. An older woman with a kind face brought me a plate heaped with a little of everything. I thanked her with one of the words I knew in Spanish. Rachel's mother ignored me, and Rachel herself sat among the women when it came their time to eat.

The shade moved, and people shifted their chairs along with it. As I looked around, I did not see Rachel's father in the company. I knew him by sight, a man with large, dark eyes and a twirling mustache, so it was easy to see he wasn't present. I also remembered his name, and hers—Escotillo. He worked as a freighter, so I figured he was off on a job somewhere. He wasn't quite the subservient type that Mora and others were—the men who worked for Whipple, for example—and I imagined

Rachel's joke about gambling and horse racing came from his side of the family.

After everyone had eaten and the plates were stacked, the women cleared away the food and the dirty dishes. Then came the cake. The frosting was thick and heavy and not very sweet, and the rest was dry without much taste. I thought I had eaten cake like that before, but I couldn't remember when. What the cake lacked in sweetness, the punch made up for. It was a combination of watery fruit juice, from buffalo berry or something like that, and a sludge of coarse sugar. Remembering my father's advice about what to do when in Rome, I drank it down.

The party began to break up at about four in the afternoon. I was ready to go, as I had spoken very little to anyone and had hardly seen Rachel. I stood up and waited as Dunbar listened to a man who was telling a story. I didn't follow his line of talk, but I gathered he was telling about some work he did. Time and again he made a tying motion and a toss, as if he was tying bundles of wheat or shocks of corn. When the man finished, Dunbar stood up and said something that looked and sounded like he was ready to go. He shook hands with the men, including Mr. Mora and the two from the ditch crew, and took his leave.

As we watered our horses at the town trough prior to leaving town, I said, "It looked like you had a full conversation with all those men."

"That's the way it is with Spanish," he said, "and I suppose any other language. Part of what you get to practice is listenin'. Do you know any other languages?"

"Just a few words of Spanish, and a few of trapper French."

"I thought maybe your father bein' a lawyer, you might know a bit of Latin."

"Not yit," I said.

I was wondering how reserved Dunbar was going to be about the visit and the conversation he had there, until that night at supper when he spilled the beans to Higgins.

"I heard something today that might be of interest," he began.

"Is that right?" said Hig, his squinty brown eyes closing in on the man who sat on his right.

"Yep. Heard it from Mora, who works for the butcher, and from a couple of Mexicans that work for our friend Whipple."

"Must be good," said Hig, "with that combination."

"I don't know how much basis there is to it, but it might be worth lookin' into."

"I guess it depends," said Hig.

"Well, Whipple's men eat beef, and Redington sells it."

"I think I knew that."

"But it seems as if, from time to time, a head of beef goes to the crew without necessarily passin' through the slaughter house. Stiver gets a receipt for it all the same, and the project gets charged for the full cost."

"That doesn't surprise me. I suppose the butcher gets a little somethin' for his trouble."

"I think so, and he doesn't always do it the same. Depending on whether the animal is branded and what kind of brand it's got, sometimes he works up a bill of sale as if he'd bought the animal, has his men kill it, and then presents a bill as a charge for the whole thing. Of course, he just gets paid his part. Other times, the animal doesn't pass through his hands. It just goes from Point A to Point B, as they say—Point A bein' somewhere out on the range, and Point B bein' the gradin' camp. The man out there gets a receipt, but for more than he pays, so he gets to skim off some for himself."

"And that's how this one deal went?"

"Seems like it. This has been goin' on for a while, and usually no one at the camp sees the meat until it's a carcass. But this time, it came in with the hide on it, and someone got a look at it."

"Had the Little Six brand on it, I'd guess."

Dunbar nodded. "From what I understood, it was a yearling heifer. Sort of a yellowish color, with dark streaks and specks on it. I'd say it was a brindle, though I didn't get a word in Spanish for it."

"Sons a bitches," said Hig. "Like I said, it doesn't surprise me a bit, but I sure don't like it. When did this one happen?"

"Within the last week, they say."

"Well, if that hide's anywhere to be found, it's as good as got the thief's mark on it."

"It would be better than trying to get those other two fellas to peach on 'em."

Odell spoke up in a loud voice. "By God," he said. "That might be what Stiver was up to the day he came spyin' on us. And that's why they hauled it back before they skinned it."

"Might be," said Hig, "but you don't know." He turned his narrow eyes to Dunbar again. "I don't know if you went out of your way to dig this up, but I appreciate you sharin' it."

"It was just somethin' that sort of came to me," said Dunbar, "and I thought you'd like to know."

Hig nodded.

"And if you want, I can look into it a little more."

"Go ahead," said Higgins. "The heifer's already gone, but if you can keep it from happenin' to any others, so much the better."

"Like they say in Spanish, he who would make one basket would make a hundred. What would you think if Grey went along?"

Hig pushed out his lower lip for a second and said, "That

would be all right."

Odell sat up straight and said, "Why don't you let me go?"

"Nah, two's enough," said Higgins. "And as for the rest of you, just keep your mouths shut about this."

Odell sat back in a slouch, but he nodded. So did Rumsey.

So did I, but I wondered why Dunbar made the discovery as public as he did. I also thought it was a small thing, this petty rustling, for him to take the trouble to go after. But then again, I didn't know what all of his reasons were or how many baskets were out there.

Dunbar was calm and unhurried as we rode into town the next day. Having taken the buckskin the day before, he was riding the blue roan. I had picked out a small, stocky sorrel, and I imagined I looked like Dunbar's junior partner as we rode through the hills and came into view of the town.

We went around the east end of the pond, crossing the stone bridge. I rode behind Dunbar and noticed him observing the earthen dam with the layer of rock protecting the base. His gaze lifted to take in the headgate, where a thin veil of water poured out. When we gained the slope on the other side, he paused long enough to cast a glance over the placid blue surface of the pond. Then we rode into town.

Redington's butcher shop sat on the north side of the main street, across from the Whitepaw Saloon and down the block on the corner. Dunbar had not said where we were going, but I was not surprised when we stopped there.

The bell tinkled as we opened the door, walked through, and closed it. Redington appeared at the counter with a businesslike "Yes, sir, how can I help you?"

He was a tall, stoop-shouldered man with dark brown hair parted in the middle. He had shadows beneath his eyes, a round nose, and a bushy mustache. He breathed with his mouth open, and with weight hanging over his belt, he often looked as if he was out of breath. At the moment, he had come out of the back area and was carrying his white butcher's apron.

"Are you Al Redington, the butcher?" asked Dunbar.

"That I am." He ducked his head forward and flipped the cloth strap of his apron over and onto his neck.

"My name's Dunbar, and I work for Bill Higgins out at the Little Six."

Redington nodded.

Dunbar took a slow breath, letting the man wait, and then said, "It looks as if there might have been an irregularity about some beef in the recent past, and he's lettin' me look into it."

The butcher tied on his apron, smoothed it out, and looked up. "I don't believe I've sold Bill Higgins any beef in a long time, if I ever did."

"Or bought some from him?"

Redington cast his eyes upward for a couple of seconds. "It's been a while since I've done any of that, as far as I recall. There are other people, closer in, who sell a head or two at a time."

"Sure." Dunbar swept his eyes along the meat case and came back to the butcher. "Would you know anything about a brindle heifer, yearling, that went on the hook last week?"

Redington gave a half-hearted laugh. "Gosh, I don't remember. I do quite a little bit of business, you know. Sometimes we run ten, twelve head a week through here, and you ask me about something that happened a week or two ago."

"Just a week."

"Well, I couldn't say for sure."

"You said you do quite a bit of business. You provide meat for the crew that's workin' on the irrigation project, don't you?"

Redington stiffened a little, and his eyes tightened. "Yes, I do, and I don't mind saying that everything's in good order."

"I'm sure it is. You keep good records of what you buy, where, and when, as well as where you sell it, I assume."

"I keep track of what I buy and who from, and I have bills for any large sales I make, but that's just quantity. If I buy a steer from Fred Miller, I don't keep track of where all the pieces went."

"But you would know whether you acquired a yearling heifer and whether that carcass went to the work camp."

Redington's eyes shifted. "Maybe not off the top of my head."

"But you would have it written down, especially if it had the Little Six brand on it."

"But it didn't. That is, I haven't bought or sold any Little Six beef. I told you that."

"And your records would show that."

Redington's eyes narrowed again. "Look, mister. I keep records, and damn good ones. But I don't have to show 'em to anyone who comes along, and I don't need you takin' up my time askin' questions that may or may not be any of your business."

"But if you had to, you could prove you didn't sell that animal."

"If it existed. But even at that, I don't have to show you anything, unless you can show me that you're some kind of a lawman."

"Well, I'm not. But one could be brought in, if there was enough of a complaint."

"We don't have that much trouble here," said Redington. "Although sometimes people try to stir it up." He seemed to be regaining his sense of authority as one of the town fathers.

Dunbar's eyebrows raised, and his face had an imperturbable expression. "I don't stir up trouble in the sense of manufacturin' it," he said, "but in the sense of bringin' it to the surface—well, you can judge for yourself. They say a watched pot never boils, but I think some pots will boil no matter how much people keep an eye on them and hope they don't."

The butcher sneered. "If you're not a lawman, you must be a philosopher, then."

"Oh, no. I'm just a cowpuncher."

Redington's condescension was back in place as he looked at me. "You ought to take an example from Grey here," he said. "I think he's got the good sense to mind his own business." He turned to Dunbar. "You're pretty inquisitive for a cowpuncher. Been that way all your life?"

"Not yit," said Dunbar.

That ended the conversation, with no pretense of being amiable on either side. I had wondered earlier why Dunbar was drawing me into this affair, and as we stepped out on the street, it occurred to me that he might have wanted to have me present as a witness, as a way of making the interview with Redington public. He was not my idea of the lone wolf stock detective, but if anything, he was methodical.

As we untied our horses, my glance drifted toward the butcher shop. Seated on a bench up against the building, where the awning shaded his face, sat a fellow I recognized. He went by the name of Brownie, and he worked for Ben Marston. How much work he did was not apparent, for he seemed to have time to loaf around town. On some occasions he drove Ben Marston's carriage, but for the most part I think he was a gatekeeper in a place that did not have a gate or a gatehouse. It was said that he slept armed and fully clothed on a couch in Marston's front room whenever the boss was in town. I believed it, because in addition to wearing a brown bowler hat, he always wore a brown corduroy coat with a shoulder holster not very well concealed beneath it.

Dunbar and I mounted up and rode a short way to the town well, where we stopped to water the horses before leaving. The day was getting into late morning, and the sun was warming things up. We were in the next lot over from the site where Dornick and his crew were working on the bank.

Dunbar gazed at them for a few minutes and said, "Looks like hot work, up against those stone walls."

"It does."

"Always worth the while to take a minute and watch others work."

"I suppose."

He took off his tall-crowned hat and set it on his saddle horn, then rolled up the sleeves of his shirt. He motioned toward the pump, so I worked the handle as he rubbed his hands together and then splashed water on his face. After he wiped his eyes and smoothed his mustache, he stood up straight. As he shook his hands and held them out to the sunlight, I saw again the spot in his hand. As before, I had the impression that he had been burned there.

"That was good," he said. "Thanks. You care to rinse off?"

I shook my head. "That's all right. I'll wait."

He turned his gaze toward the bank again. "Makes me hot to look at it," he remarked. "All those materials—rock, mortar, cement—they hold heat and reflect it. That's why the downtown of a city gets like an oven on a hot summer day. You ever been to Chicago?"

"No."

"Well, it's a good one for gettin' hotter 'n hell. Stay away from there in the summer. Winter, too, as far as that goes."

"I'll remember that."

He put the dark hat back on his head and pulled on his gloves. "I guess we can go now."

When we got to the hills south of town, he pointed the roan to the trail that led southwest in the direction of the water project. I wondered if anyone would try to get out there ahead of us, but I doubted it. I imagined that when people made deals like the ones that seemed to have gone on here, the two parties had it worked out in case any questions came up.

We rode through the grassland, which seemed to be getting drier and more brittle by the day. My sorrel picked up his feet to stay alongside Dunbar's roan. A light breeze stirred, and bits of broken grass lifted in the whirls and eddies as we went.

"This is good country," said Dunbar. "Do you think you'll stay with it?"

"I haven't thought about it very much one way or the other, but I don't have plans to leave."

"Some people, they grow up around a little town, and they can't wait to get to a big one. Others, they grow up in a place and it stays in their blood."

"I'm probably more like the latter."

"Others, they go from one place to another. Even then, they're not the same. For some, the grass is always greener somewhere else, and they won't do any better wherever they go. Then there's those that follow their work. Do a job in one place and then move on to the next."

I thought he might be talking about himself, but then it occurred to me that he might be thinking of someone like Whipple.

"That never interested me," I said. "I'd rather belong somewhere."

"It's a good way to be." After about a minute he spoke again. "By the way, do you know why they call this town Winsome?"

" 'Win some and lose some,' is what Manfred says."

"Means young and innocent, too."

"I know. My father had a dictionary."

"I should have thought of that."

I thought he might be trying to draw me out on something and then gave up, but I didn't know. We rode on for another hour without saying much. Sometimes Dunbar muttered a syllable or two to his horse, and sometimes I spoke to mine. Out in the middle of that grassland, it was not hard to imagine how someone on a distant hill would see us, a senior partner and a junior, jogging along on mismatched horses.

The sun was straight up when we crested a hill and paused to take a look at the work site. A mile away, scratches showed in the earth where scrapers had shaved away the sage and grass. I could see the dam beginning to take shape across the mouth of the canyon, and I knew it had taken hundreds if not thousands of scraper loads just to form the base. Farther back, in the clefts of the canyon, dark cedars clung to the sides while cottonwoods, chokecherries, and alders grew in the drainage. It occurred to me that when the project was done, some of that growth would be under water.

"Lot of work," said Dunbar.

"Yeah."

"They say when Ferdinand de Lesseps dug the Suez Canal, he had thousands of men, Egyptians like the ones who built the pyramids, and one after another they filled up baskets of dirt and carried 'em out of there. Took 'em ten years. You look at this, and you can imagine how much bigger that other job was. From what they say, there's big projects on the way in this country, too."

"It takes more than what I've got," I said.

"Me, too. Even if it's not the master-and-slave method, I've got no knack for it."

Chapter Five

From a distance, the men and horses on the work project looked like so many insects, indistinguishable from one another and not making any noise that I could hear. The work itself was familiar to me, so I didn't have the sensation of dropping into an empire of a distant time and place, as I imagined those of the Egyptians and Incas to be, with legions of slaves and their armed overseers. All the same, the scene had an aura of strangeness as men and horses and equipment scarified the earth and changed its features. I had seen pits and cellars dug before, and I had seen the reservoir at Winsome take shape, but I had not seen defacement, or disfigurement, on such a large scale.

The long mound of dirt that would be the base of the dam ran for over a quarter of a mile southeast-northwest, with its end points touching rises in the earth where the ground sloped from the base of the bluffs to the level area of the plain. Men with teams of horses pulling scrapers were moving dirt from the floor of the reservoir to the dam, and so far an area of nearly two hundred acres had been torn up.

In addition to that, two teams had begun cutting the ditch and were making crosswise movements of going down into the bed, scraping a load, dragging it up on the bank, and dumping it. I could see it was going to be a canal several yards across, not the kind of ditch one might imagine at hearing the word. Ditches I had seen were more like trenches, being dug by a line of men bending over with picks and shovels. But in this new era of water projects, what some people called a canal went by the name of ditch.

To the south of the whole work area sat the camp. It looked like other work camps I have seen, with an assortment of canvas shacks and piles of materials. This one had what looked like about a dozen sleeping tents, one larger tent for cook shack and mess, a stack of lumber, another of bulging grain sacks, a pyramid of wooden kegs, a huddle of steel barrels, half a dozen wagons, and a five-acre barbed-wire holding pen where a dozen work animals stood dozing in the midday sun.

At least twenty men and that many horses and mules were crawling to and fro on the work site. As Dunbar and I rode closer, I was able to pick out some workers I knew and some animals I recognized. Stiver was easy to identify because of his cap that looked like a muffin. His yellowish-white horse loitered in the pasture with the others, so he was on foot, standing on a high spot on the south end of the long berm of dirt.

Out of the dust and movement emerged Tut Whipple, his blond hair and mustache visible at a quarter of a mile. He was carrying a scroll of paper in one hand and a shovel in the other.

I turned to Dunbar and asked, "Where do you want to start?"

"I'd like to look around up on top," he said. "I'll leave you here to chat with your friends for a while." With that, he touched his spurs to the roan and set off to the northwest in the direction of the road that led up out of the basin and onto the Rim.

I rode forward to meet Whipple, who walked up onto the mounded dirt and stood waiting, resting the blade of the shovel on the ground and holding the handle like a staff. In his other hand, the roll of paper shone bright in the sunlight. As I dismounted, he said, "What wind brings you here today?"

I decided to let Dunbar introduce the topic of the day when he got back, so I said, "Just came out to take a look around."

He glanced in the direction where Dunbar was riding toward

the Rim. "I don't suppose you have much choice about the company you keep."

"Sometimes Hig sends us out together."

"Part of your education, huh?" Whipple put on a look of disdain. "Teach you to grow up and be a drifter, and a spy to boot."

"You think he's a spy?" I asked.

Tut wrinkled his nose. "At first I thought Higgins put him on to come snoopin'. Then it occurred to me that he might be workin' for some other investment company, spyin' on our progress, and workin' for Higgins as a cover. Either way, I don't like him ridin' here and there, gawkin' like a goony bird. Not that he can do a damn thing anyway."

I thought of goony birds as being waterfowl like grebes and loons and herons, and I didn't think of them as being gawkers, but I imagined Tut thought it was a clever thing to say. "Well, how *is* the progress?" I asked. "Moving along?"

"At a snail's pace." He waved the roll of paper at the torn-up area that was becoming a bowl, though still shallow at this point. "People in charge want this thing dug overnight. And as you know, it ain't that way."

"You've got a bigger crew here."

"Sure. Four times the crew, and ten times the work. And the more men you got, the more often you look around and see someone scratchin' his ass and not doin' anythin'."

At that moment a team of four horses, side by side, came huffing up the slope with a Fresno Scraper in tow. The man operating the scraper followed behind, holding down the handle so that the full load would skid. As the horses went over the bank, the man lifted the handle and dumped nearly a half-yard of dirt on the top of the dam. Dust rose around the edges of the pile as the team, scraper, and operator went down the bank and made a turn to go fetch another load.

"One dump at a time," I said, "but it adds up."

"By God, I'd like to have a steam shovel."

"Do you know how to operate one?"

"I don't need to. Get a man along with it. But I could learn quick enough. It's like your steam-powered grain threshers. These honyockers can learn to run 'em. Trouble is, you need a lot of work in one place to make it worthwhile to go to all the bother of bringin' in a piece of machinery that big."

I nodded. I figured, and hoped, that the wheat farmers in Decker Basin who had a hundred and sixty acres here and there would be a long time waiting to see one of those ungainly beasts.

"So the people in charge won't let you try it, then?"

"Puh," said Whipple in a dry spit. "They don't care if I do it all with a shovel and a wheelbarrow." He pointed the end of the scroll of paper at his chest. "I'm the contractor. I sign on to do the work, and I get it done the best way I know how, and as quick as I can." He lifted his head and tossed it in a bit of a swagger. "Thing is, I don't have the capital. If I brought in a steam shovel, I'd have to have another big job to go to, to make it pay."

"I see." Another team came up the slope twenty yards away and dumped a load. "How high do you have to build this?" I asked.

"Another fourteen, fifteen feet."

"Whew. That's a lot of dirt."

"You're damn right it is."

"And what kind of a gate are you planning to put in?"

"It'll be a cement box, a hell of a lot bigger than the wooden one we put in on that little pond. Then there'll be a wooden box, or frame, inside that, with overhead beams and then planks to raise and lower the flow. We'll have a rock wall on either side and running across underneath. Rocks set in cement, you know—nothing fancy, because a good part of it'll be under water most of the time."

I tried to picture it, plastered into a huge bank of dirt above where I was now standing.

"I'll have Dornick do the masonry," he went on. "Box and everything. He calls it a weir, you know."

"Oh, yeah. That's what he called the other one."

"I don't care what he calls it, as long as he gets it built."

I let my gaze drift back into the canyon. "No shortage of rock, anyway."

"Oh, no. Just a matter of movin' it." He wagged his head again, as if he were the patron. "Got another crew comin' in to take out firewood. No sense in lettin' it all go under water."

"Don't you need it for your camp?"

He turned down the corners of his mouth. "It's all green. Won't be any good 'til next year. We've got all the dry stuff out already."

"That's good."

"Oh, yeah." Whipple stopped short. "What the hell's he doin' up there?"

I raised my eyes and saw Dunbar riding along the rim of the bluff. From his posture I guessed he was looking down into the canyon. "I don't know," I said.

Another scraper, this one with a two-horse team, came up onto the mound and left a deposit.

"So how many outfits do you have moving dirt?" I asked.

"Four with four horses and that one with two. Of course, there's no end to the pick-and-shovel work."

"Oh, yeah." I saw two men grubbing out sagebrush with mattocks and tossing the brush into a wagon. "Little bit of everything."

"Pretty soon we'll start movin' rock. Wish I had a machine for that, too. It all takes time."

"Sure." Now Stiver in his cloth cap and brown suspenders

was walking down the slope into the work area. He stopped where the two men were working with mattocks, and I could tell he was doing what he did best—bossing around the help. He pointed at the sagebrush and then at the wagon. The two men nodded.

"I'd like to have about half a dozen young fellas like you," Whipple said. "We'd get that rock moved then."

"Wear out a few pair of leather gloves," I said. "If I was going to do that kind of work again, I think I'd wear chaps as well." I remembered the twelve-pound sledge, with the rock dust stuck to the head, and all the rough pieces. "Not in a hurry to do it, though."

"I don't blame you. I think I might hire a couple of more Mexicans for that. Get a crew of four. They work all right together, as long as you keep after 'em."

Now his gaze went upward again, and I followed it. There was Dunbar, having ridden around to the south wall of the canyon. He was silhouetted against the sky as he sat on the blue roan horse and looked down at the men and work.

Tut made a hissing sound. "I don't like him ridin' here and there and wherever he damn well pleases. You don't have any idea what he's up to?"

"Not up there," I said.

"Well, I wish to hell he'd stay away. Better yet, go back to where he came from. I've got work to do, and I don't need him distractin' my men."

I shrugged. I was thinking I should say something when a faint tinkle sounded in the direction of camp. Right away, men relayed the call to one another. "Dinner! Dinner! Dinner!" I imagined Dunbar could hear the voices from up above, but he kept his place as the men left off their work and began to trudge toward camp. The men running scrapers kept at it, and I knew they would each finish the load they were on and would begin unhitching.

"Do you have a horse here?" I asked Tut.

"No," he answered, in a tone that suggested I was a loafer. "We walk." He stabbed the shovel into the loose dirt and turned around.

"That's all right," I said. With my reins loose and my horse trailing, I fell in beside Tut Whipple and walked toward the work camp.

I was sorry to miss the three-hundred-pound cook who was said to have run the camp before. In his place, I found a big-nosed, glassy-eyed man of middle height. I guessed him to be in his middle fifties, as his hair had thinned on top and his belly sagged. He had spindly arms and a slack chest, so that in profile, the slope of his knobby nose was paralleled, on a larger scale, with the slope of his soft belly. His name was Pete, and I saw soon enough that he didn't do much of the work himself but delegated it to his camp helper, a shorter, white-haired man named Nat. Pete stood by looking like a benevolent uncle while Nat scurried among the pots and dishes.

As I came from tying up my horse, Pete gave me a big smile and said, in a loud voice, "Well, it looks like we've got company. Nat, water down the soup and dig out an extra plate."

Tut and I got in line behind half a dozen workers. As the men ahead served themselves out of the cast-iron kettles, I saw that the main dish of the day was beef stew. The line moved along past the pots hanging over the coals, and at the end, each man took biscuits from a table. The men sat on the ground, cross-legged, in no particular order. I sat on the ground as well, but Tut waited until Nat brought him a camp chair.

I hadn't been eating for long when one of the other men piped up. "Rider comin'."

It was Dunbar, who swung down and walked his horse in for thirty yards. I looked at Whipple and saw that his face had gone rigid, but I knew no one would go against the custom of the country. A man who came into camp, even if he was a bitter rival, ate with everyone else.

Dunbar no doubt counted on it, as he tied his horse to a wagon wheel not far from mine and headed toward the iron rack over the fire pit.

Pete spoke again in his loud voice, which had a bit of a quack to it. "Get a plate from Nat, stranger, and help yourself. Stew's in the pot."

In his untroubled manner, Dunbar served up a tin plate of stew and grabbed a couple of biscuits. He walked over to where I sat and found a spot between me and a worker I knew from before named Ingraham. Dunbar and Whipple seemed to ignore each other, which I thought was convenient for the moment.

The two Mexicans we had seen at the fiesta sat not far away, and I appreciated how neither they nor Dunbar showed any recognition of one another.

Ingraham, who would have no reason to know that Whipple harbored a dislike for Dunbar, started in with his usual chatter. "Where you from, stranger? You're the fella that was up on the rim a little while ago, aren't you?"

"That's right," said Dunbar. "It was me. My name's Dunbar, and I work with Grey at the Little Six."

"Then you know Rumsey and Odell."

"Sure do."

"How long you been here?"

"Oh, a couple of weeks, I'd say."

"Is that right? How long do you think you'll stay? You've got fall roundup comin' up, haven't you?"

"That's right."

"Lotta work here. We'll go past that, I'm sure. Can't dig when the ground's froze, though."

"I imagine."

"Seen much of the country north of here?"

"Not yet."

"They say it's different."

"Might be."

"The farther you get from the mountains, the less water you get."

"Sometimes." Dunbar stretched his back. "Depends on the part of the country."

"I guess it does. They say if you go to the Platte and follow it upriver to the west, or the northwest, there's places all along there where they can put in dams."

"I wouldn't be surprised."

"There's gonna be a lot of work in this country for a long time."

"That's good. Times have been rough the last few years, not much money."

Ingraham laughed. "Oh, I never said any of this paid much. But there's work, and there will be, for them that want to do it."

Dunbar ate without speaking. Ingraham, who had gotten a good start and ate as fast as he talked, set his empty plate aside. He was a common-looking fellow, with beady eyes, a stubbled face, and a filmy complexion. He wore a short-brimmed hat with a low, round crown, and it was as dusty as the rest of him—his shirt of coarse cotton, his old denim trousers cuffed at the bottom, and his clodhopper boots. For all his grubby appearance, though, he did his work, and I found his company more tolerable than Stiver's.

Now that he was finished eating, he took out a plug of tobacco and a jackknife, and he cut himself a chaw. When he worked it into his cheek and had his first spit, he was ready to talk again. "Seen you up on the bluffs," he began. "Looked like you were lookin' for somethin'."

"Kind of. Hard to look for somethin' you've got only a hazy idea about."

"Oh, I imagine. What would that be, or is it somethin' I shouldn't ask?"

"Oh, no harm," said Dunbar. "Just a matter of speculation anyway."

"Is that right? If there's anything out here except ticks and rattlesnakes, I'd be surprised."

Dunbar finished a mouthful and then answered. "Well, you know, you see a lot of this country that looks like it's never been touched. Makes you think you're the first ones ever stopped here. You sit on a rock in that canyon, and you wonder if anyone ever sat on it before. You've had notions like that, haven't you?"

Ingraham moved his head side to side, as if he was weighing the idea. "I guess."

"I know I've thought that way, anyway. But everyone knows the Indians were all over this place for a long time. They just didn't leave much sign."

"Crew I was on one time dug up an Indian wrapped in a blanket. That was down in Kansas. Fella I was with said it was a blanket the army give out, so he wasn't there all that long. Twenty years, maybe."

"Could be," said Dunbar. "What I've heard is that in this part of the country, there's old Indian caves in a lot of these bluffs and buttes. In some of 'em, they're supposed to have stashed their dead people."

"I wouldn't doubt it. Easier 'n diggin' a hole."

Nat came around with a big black enamel coffee pot and a cluster of tin cups, and he poured each of us a cup of coffee. He avoided looking at me, but I observed his red eyes and pointed purplish nose. When he moved on, Dunbar spoke again.

"Now, in these places where they plan to back water up into

a canyon, there's a chance they might flood some of those caves."

"Shouldn't matter much," said Ingraham. "Those people are long gone, and so are the ones that put 'em there." He glanced at the bluffs. "And the water's not goin' to go very high up on those walls anyway."

"No, but once the water's in there, it'll make it hard to get at any of the caves whether they're flooded or not."

Ingraham spit out a squirt of tobacco juice. "What would someone want to do that for, anyway? None of these Indians buried treasure with the dead ones, did they?"

"Not that I know of. But there could be a lot of other artifacts that museums would be interested in. And they pay money for that stuff."

I noticed that some of the other workers were paying attention. A few had shifted in their seats on the ground, and Dunbar had an audience of eight or ten when he mentioned money. At the periphery stood Pete, the cook, whose voice had a quack to it again as he spoke up.

"I've had some experience at that, collecting arrowheads and the like. You can pick 'em up all over the place, and they're not worth a dollar a dozen. I can't believe you're wasting your time on it."

Dunbar looked up with a calm expression. "What else would I be looking for?"

I caught a glimpse of Tut Whipple, whose face was strained.

"I have no idea," chirped the cook.

Dunbar looked around at the men seated on the ground. Returning to Ingraham, he said, "Anyway, there might be something of value in one of these caves. I'll admit I'm selfish and would like to get it first, but I'd rather see someone else get it than no one at all. And to tell the truth, maybe one of you will lead me to it. Chance I take, but I want to beat the clock, make sure there's nothin' in this canyon before the water rises and keeps anyone from findin' it."

"Sounds like you're comin' around to somethin'," said Ingraham.

"It might not be this canyon. It might be one of the others. But the information I got has made me think it's this one."

"Information? What kind?"

"It might be like a lot of other stories," Dunbar answered, "but I know part of it is true." He took a sip of coffee. "I know for a fact that seventeen years ago, someone robbed a stagecoach over on the road between Chugwater and Bordeaux. Whoever did it came up out of that valley, across the flats, and down off the rim into one of these places."

"And they stashed the money?"

"Supposed to have hidden it in one of these Indian caves."

"They never came back for it?"

Dunbar gave Ingraham a direct look. "Not yet. They're still in the pen in Laramie."

"How can you be so sure of all this?"

"Let's just say I know one of 'em."

By now Stiver had drifted over and stood near Pete. "This sounds like a bunch of horse shit to me," he said.

Dunbar raised his eyes to meet Stiver. "Why do you say that?"

"There's no hidden gold out here."

"I didn't say there was gold."

"Well, whatever kind of money it's supposed to be. If it's really there, why would you come in and tell everyone about it?"

Dunbar shrugged. "I can't very well come into the middle of your work project and rummage around without giving some account."

"You can rummage all you want and not find a nickel, but I don't think that's what you're up to."

Dunbar smiled. "If that's the case, I can ask you what I asked the cook. What else would I be looking for?"

"Trouble," said Stiver. "I think someone sent you in here to stir up trouble, try to get my men to go off on wild goose chases instead of tendin' to their work."

"Who would want me to do a thing like that?"

"Damned if I know, but I know you're up to somethin'."

"Think again, then, about what it might be."

By now, just about everyone in the work camp had gathered around. Red-eyed Nat was sitting on a bench farther back, eating his dinner, and beyond him, two men were brushing horses. Someone might have gone into one of the tents, but more than fifteen men were watching and listening.

Stiver cocked his head back. "I don't like you comin' in here and startin' trouble. I don't care what you say you're looking for. I say it's horse shit."

"There's somethin' I haven't mentioned yet. We'll see what you have to say about that."

"Well, spit it out. We haven't got all day. Some of us have work to do."

"Hope you don't mind if I stand." Dunbar rose to his feet so that he faced Stiver and had Whipple on his left. "Here it is, then. I came to ask about some beef that might not have been on the up-and-up."

Stiver's eyes narrowed and his face hardened. "Oh, you're all wet," he said.

Dunbar went on as if the man had said nothing. "Yearling heifer with a Little Six brand. I've traced it to you, and for all I know, that's some of what we all had for dinner."

"Oh, go on. You've got no proof."

"I can get some."

"Show me the hide."

"It may be around. You might have buried it, or you might have disposed of it by some other means. But you had it. Brindle hide with a Little Six brand. Went through your hands."

"That's a lie."

Silence fell on the whole group until Dunbar answered. "You're goin' to have to back that up."

"I will," said Stiver. "Take off your gun." He began unbuckling his own.

"See here," said Pete. "I won't have any fighting in my camp."

"Shut up and hold this," said Stiver, handing him the gunbelt. "It won't take long."

All the men who had been sitting rose to their feet. I was among them, and Dunbar handed me his belt and holster, then his hat.

Stiver had taken off his cloth cap, and he stood in his dull white shirt sleeves with his fists up. He was of medium height with broad shoulders, and he had a reputation for being good with his dukes, but I wondered if his judgment hadn't been clouded for a moment. Dunbar was half a head taller, husky and trim in his wool vest, and his hands did not look dainty as they came up in fists.

Stiver moved in on short steps and tried to bat down his opponent's guard, first with his right and then with his left. He didn't have success, but he followed through anyway, leading with his left foot and trying to land a straight-arm punch to the jaw.

Dunbar knocked the fist upward and came back with a left that made Stiver's hair shake. Then he came around with a right that connected and sent the man stepping backward.

Stiver regained his footing, put up his guard, and came forward looking to throw a punch. As he moved in, Dunbar stunned him with a left jab, then came across with a right that turned Stiver's head and brought blood to his mouth. Dunbar did not stop. He inched forward, giving Stiver a left, right, left, and then delivered a jarring right that sent Stiver to the ground.

Whipple leaned to help him up. "Are you all right, Mick?"

"Yeah, yeah. I can take him." Stiver came to his feet but did not bring his guard up. His eyebrows were lifted wide, but his eyelids were half-closed.

Whipple shook his head. "I think you've had enough, Mick."

"Hell if I have."

Dunbar stood waiting, and when Stiver raised his fists and came forward, Dunbar stepped in and floored him with a right. "Listen to your boss," said Dunbar. "That's enough."

"Enough of everything," said Whipple. "Just get out. You come in here startin' trouble, and—"

"He said it was a lie. He knew better, but he thought he could save face."

Whipple's own face was tight, and his jaw muscle was bulging. "You didn't prove anythin'," he said. "That is, nothin' you came to prove."

Dunbar reached for his hat, and I handed it to him. As he put it on, he said, "I'm not through yet."

"If you were smart, you would be. But I wouldn't give you credit for being smart."

"I don't need credit from you," Dunbar answered, "and I don't think we keep the same kind of ledger anyway."

An uncertain expression passed over Whipple's face until he got his authority back. "Don't come here again," he said.

"I may not have to." Dunbar held his hand toward me, and I gave him his gunbelt.

As he buckled it on, I got a view of a few men who had not yet turned away. The two Mexicans had no expression at all, but they had taken in every detail. So had Ingraham, whose eyes were open in a stare. Pete the cook gazed at Stiver with no sympathy, as if he was relieved that someone else had taken the pummeling. Only Tut Whipple looked as if he dared resent what had happened, but I didn't see him ready to do anything about it at the moment.

Chapter Six

Dunbar and I did not ride together for the next several days. Hig let him come and go on his own, and I derived the sense that they had an unspoken agreement for Dunbar to keep an eye on the ditch crew and see if they were rustling beef or pulling some other shenanigan. Whenever I was out on the range and saw the Rim in the distance, with its pale shining bluffs and shadowy folds, I wondered what kinds of secrets, if any, were to be found there, and I wondered if Dunbar would find them out.

I went into town by myself about a week after the fight between Dunbar and Stiver. I entered town on the east side of the pond, crossing the stone bridge and noting the thin stream of water pouring out of the headgate, then climbing the slope and gazing for a moment at the calm blue surface of the pond.

I turned right on the main street. Dornick's crew was working on the other side of the bank building, so I did not see the stone mason. I saw one of his men pushing a wheelbarrow out of sight. I rode onward, passing the town well and water trough on my left, and crossed the next street. Past the heap of rubble on my right, I came to the Castle and turned in.

Four horses that looked as if they had come in from the range stood hipshot at the hitching rail. I tied mine a few feet away, noted the dry boards of the cistern, and went into the tavern.

At the bar, four cowboys stood talking and laughing. I thought I recognized a couple of them from farther south, down by Horse Creek, and I wondered what they were doing up this way. Then, as if I heard my father's voice, I told myself it wasn't any of my business. I went to the end of the bar nearest the kitchen, laid a silver dollar on the bar top, and listened for voices.

Clark the proprietor came to wait on me. "What'll it be?" he asked.

"A glass of beer." As he turned away and tended to my order, I listened again for voices in the kitchen and heard none.

Clark set the beer in front of me but did not touch the coin.

"Go ahead and take out for it now," I said. "I'm going to have just one." When he brought my change, I asked, "Slow day in the kitchen?"

"She's not here."

"Not any more, or just today?"

He lowered his chin, and the folds beneath it spread out. "She's not here today." He turned and went back to his stool near the cashbox. It looked as if he put pressure on his guts when he sat that way, and a minute later I heard him make his sound of coughing up from the bottom of his throat.

I settled into my own company and enjoyed my beer. The cowpunchers down the bar were having a good time. The liveliest one in the group was doing voice imitations and getting lots of laughs. He also did a good rendition of a coyote's yip and howl. The other fellows called him Dakota, and after a little while they coaxed him into singing. He did one short ditty about meeting Sally behind the outhouse, and then he sang a longer song that I had never heard before. I think it was called "Jim Weston Isn't Dead," and it went like this:

Was the talk throughout the barroom
Where the worst of rumors spread
That a puncher from among us
Named Jim Weston was now dead.

'Twas the middle of November
When the roundup was all done,
All the steers were in the boxcars,
It was time to have some fun.

So our crew of twenty cowboys
Took a fast lope into town.
But we saw when we dismounted
That Jim Weston wasn't around.

"Now where the hell's he gone to?"
Asked his saddle pard named Max.
"I was sure he was among us
When we started makin' tracks."

No one had a ready answer
'Cept a man named Nat the Rat,
Who had never cinched a saddle,
Never worn a Stetson hat.

In the comfort of the barroom
With a glass half-full of gin,
He was pleased to comment lightly
On the life of our pal Jim.

"Oh, he probably took a detour
So that he could get here first.
He most likely took a tumble
And is out there in the dirt.

"That's the way with all these cowboys,
They can't wait to get to town,
So they ride hell-bent and reckless
Till their pony throws 'em down.

"So I wouldn't fret about it,
Save your tears, don't waste your breath,
'Cause if his neck ain't broken,
Then he's probably froze to death."

Well, the first to give rejoinder
Was our pal named Marble Mike.
He replied, "I don't think Weston's
Quite as dead as you would like."

"Oh, no one said he wished it,"
Answered Big Nose Pete the wit.
"But if Weston's dead, why doubt it?
There's no shame in sayin' it."

Then the next to speak was Johnny,
Who'd been Weston's pal for years.
He said, "Me 'n' Bob 'n' Dusty's
Got a hunch where Weston is."

"Weston's dead," said Pete the Parrot,
In refrain with Nat the Rat.
"But if you think you know different,
You can tell us where he's at."

Johnny poured a drink of whiskey,
Set his hat back on his head,
Looked around at his companions,
And to all who doubted said:

"Those of us that's ridden with him
Know Jim Weston isn't dead.
He's just holed up in his cabin
Snug and cozy in his bed,

"With a blond-haired gal named Susie,
Who will keep him warm and fed.
So don't worry 'bout Jim Weston
'Cause he's nowhere close to dead."

Now you'd think that would have clinched it,
But the talk went on and on,
All about our friend Jim Weston
And if he was dead and gone.

As for me, I think Jim Weston
Is untouched by all this noise
And he wouldn't mind my singin'
'Long with Johnny and the boys:

"Those of us that's ridden with him
Know Jim Weston isn't dead.
He's just holed up in his cabin
Snug and cozy in his bed,

"With a blond-haired gal named Susie,
Who will keep him warm and fed.
So don't worry 'bout Jim Weston
'Cause he's nowhere close to dead."

When the singer came to the refrain, his three pals joined in. Then they did the song a couple of more times, and by the time they finished, I had it pretty well in my head. They were a jolly bunch, young and loose and carefree, and it did me good to see them having fun.

When I finished my beer, I went out into the bright sunlight and untied my horse. The cowboys from down by Horse Creek were starting in on the Jim Weston song again as I swung up into the saddle and rode away.

After two blocks, I dismounted and tied up in front of the Whitepaw Saloon. I walked inside and paused to let my eyes adjust. As I looked around I saw the bobcat with his white paw raised, and then my line of sight traveled to the painting where the Indian brave knelt straddling his conquest. The two images served to reassure me, as they often did, that not much changed in the Whitepaw Saloon.

Familiar voices brought my gaze to rest on the group of four men who sat at their customary table. There was Fenn Fuller, with his bowler hat hanging on the post in back of him. At his left sat Lon Buckley, the proprietor, with his wavy gray hair, light-colored vest, and white shirt with arm garters. Sitting away from the table, turned and somewhat in a slouch, sat Henry Dornick. His right hand reached out for the mug of beer on the table, and his left hand cupped the bowl of the curved-stem pipe he was smoking. On his left side and Fenn's right, also turned so that he did not have his back to the door, sat Al Redington, bulky in contrast with the slender stone mason in loose-fitting clothes.

Fenn Fuller's voice rose on the air. "Well, look who came in. Have a seat, boy." He waved at the table.

Although there was more space between Dornick and Redington, I did not want to sit with my back to the door, and as a lesser consideration I would just as soon not sit close to Redington, the butcher. Therefore I pulled a chair around and sat between Dornick, who straightened in his seat, and Buckley, who signaled to his bartender Herb to bring me a beer.

Fenn Fuller had a glass of brandy in front of him and seemed to enjoy his position as always. He resumed a topic that I assumed had been in progress when I came in. "He's got credit, but if he keeps pushin' it to the limit, he may find himself doin' what so many others do—packin' up and startin' over in a new place, sellin' his wares on a plank bench inside a tent."

"Not so much different from what he does here," said Redington.

I guessed they were talking about the man who ran the general store. He had come to town a year earlier, and a few of the other merchants were jealous because he sold some of the same goods as they did. I imagined him in a tent city, selling bacon and flour and canned tomatoes on a plank counter set up on barrels.

"A man is as good as his word," Fenn went on. "If you tell a man you're going to pay him on Monday, you shouldn't leave him guessin' which Monday. Anythin' that gets freighted into this town has got to be paid for. None of it is free. When you pay a man up, he knows you're good to do business with." Fenn patted the backs of his right fingers in the palm of his left hand.

"That's right," said Redington. "We're expected to carry men until they get their crops in or sell their cattle, but if we turned around and did the same thing, told our suppliers to wait 'til November to be paid for their canned goods, cloth, or hardware—why, it's just no good. I go through more than a side of bacon every week, about six a month, and I pay right up. This other fella, he gets his bacon in the same place, and he leaves 'em waitin'. I know, because they tell me."

"You hit it right," said Fenn. "We're expected to carry all these people, and I don't mind it. It's what they expect out of someone who's stable and they know he's got a stake in seein' things through in this town. People come and go. Some of 'em are fly-by-nighters, and some of 'em go broke slowly, but we're the ones who stick it out and try to make something better out of the town while we do it."

"You think he'll go broke, then?" asked Buckley.

"Oh, I don't know." Fenn adjusted his spectacles. "Don't want to wish anything bad on anyone, but a man should—well, no need to say what I've already said." His eyes came around to me, and he had a cheery pose as he spoke. "And what's new out your way?"

"Not much," I said.

"Pastures dryin' up?"

"Little by little."

Buckley spoke up again. "Is that fellow Dunbar still around?"

"Last I knew. Unless he left since I came into town."

"I heard he had a little run-in. Not that I mind who he did it to, but he could wear out his welcome. What's Hig think of it?"

"I don't know. I go about my own work."

"Sure," said Buckley.

Redington spoke next. "Well, I didn't like the way he came around makin' insinuations. He does that in the wrong way, he'll do more than wear out his welcome. And I guess he did the same thing out there at the camp. What's he think he's doin'?"

Fenn had taken out his watch and now paused with it in his hand. "Let's not blame it on Grey," he said. "He's not the man's keeper."

Dornick may have wanted to change the subject, as he said, "How are things around town?" He settled on Redington. "How about your man Mora, Al? Any word on his daughter?"

"Nah." The butcher shook his head. "Nothin' seems to change. Except maybe with you. You're gettin' things done, I can see that."

Dornick shrugged. "Doin' our work. Sometimes it shows more than at others."

Fenn smiled, and his ruddy cheeks were shiny. "That's how a town makes progress. If everyone did his work, there would be a lot less problems."

"Is there anyone in town who isn't?" I asked.

"Oh, I don't know," said Fenn, opening his eyes wide. He nodded at Dornick and then Redington as he said, "Your men do their work, that's plain to see, and your men do theirs."

My voice seemed to come out by itself. "I wonder if anyone will ever find out what happened to the Mora girl."

Fenn gave me a close look as he put his watch away. "Do you mean it should be someone's job and they're not doing it?"

"I don't know what I mean," I admitted. "I just wonder."

His face relaxed. "I can't blame you, boy. I'm sure we all wonder about things. But it's hard for anyone to do somethin' when you don't know if there's a reason. You've got to have probable cause, you know, not just go around assuming things."

"That's for damn sure," said Redington. "We've had enough of that."

Fenn put on the smile of the benevolent uncle. "But I'll tell you, Grey, if I knew—that is, if we knew—there was cause, something would be done." He looked around the table. "Any of us will tell you the same thing. You can't sit around and hope someone else will take it upon himself. Like that fellow with the two crib girls. We took care of that ourselves, told him we didn't need that here. He packed up and left."

Buckley gave a shrug. "Can't say that every cowpuncher agreed, but they know where else they can go."

His face and gray hair brightened as the front door opened. We all looked in that direction as the shapes of two tall men filled the doorway. The men came inside, and as the door closed I saw that one of them was Tut Whipple. The other I did not recognize.

They walked forward, passed our table, and strode to the bar. There, each of them drew up to his full height, raised his chin, and looked around. It looked as if they were doing a tall-man strut and enjoyed doing it together. Above them the Indian warrior crouched, forever poised, but they did not look at him. They surveyed what little crowd was at the bar.

"Wonder who that is with Whipple," said Buckley. "I believe

he's new in town."

"I'd guess it's someone Tut brought in," Redington offered. "Every time I've talked to him, he's said he needed to step things up."

My words came out again. "Trying to beat the clock."

Fenn Fuller looked at me as if I had spoken out of place. "Can't blame a man for tryin' to get his work done, if that's what he's doin'."

"Oh, no," I said. "I know."

Dornick laughed and patted me on the arm. "Sure you know. You worked for him. He was tryin' to beat the clock even then."

Fenn smiled, and his reddish-silver side-whiskers pushed out. "He got his work done, Whipple did. And every man's labor contributed to it."

When I left the Whitepaw Saloon, I went through town with the intention of stopping to see Ruth. I rode past the building where my father's law office had been and where his books still sat on shelves. I thought of the itinerant lawyer who came through town every month or so, and then I thought no more of that business. I turned left and went to Ruth's house, where no answer came to my knock at the door. I knocked again and called out, but I got no response, so I left town and rode to the ranch.

I found Manfred in a good mood, singing a single line over and over as he rolled out the dough for biscuits. It had a bouncy tune: *"We will not serve potato soup today."*

After he had sung it four or five times, I asked him where it came from.

"I don't know," he said. "It just came into my head, and if I don't sing it out, it'll stay there trapped. Maybe I can pass it on to you."

"I hope not." I watched him roll the dough a couple of times and then said, "By the way, when I was in town, I heard a song that referred to Big Nose Pete and Nat the Rat. Would those be the same two that run the camp for Tut Whipple's crew?"

"Could be. I didn't know they were out there. I barely know 'em by sight. Last I heard, they were workin' for a cow outfit east of Iron Mountain quite a ways."

"That's probably it. I thought I recognized a couple of the punchers who were singing this song. Seemed to me they were from down by Horse Creek."

"That would be it."

"The song was about a man named Jim Weston. Do you know who he is?"

Manfred shook his head. "Never heard of him."

"Well, I've got that tune jangling through my head."

"You can try replacing it with another." He set the rolling pin aside and looked at me. "What's new in town?"

"Not much. Looks as if Tut Whipple brought in a new man. Saw 'em both in the saloon."

"What's he look like?"

"Tall duck."

Manfred began cutting out biscuits with the mouth of an empty can. "What I mean is, does he look like a ditch grader, or does he look like someone brought in to do what Stiver couldn't?"

"I don't know. He could be either or both."

He cut out the rest of the biscuits and rolled up the leftover dough. As he did, he rubbed at a smidgin of dough that had stuck to the palm of his hand.

"Say, I've got a question," I said.

"What is it?" He didn't look up from rolling the dough back and forth on the counter.

"I've noticed a couple of times that Dunbar has what looks like a burned spot in the palm of his right hand."

The cook shrugged. "Haven't noticed it."

"Well, I've seen it more than once, and it's dark, like it was branded there."

"Maybe it was."

"It's none of my business, but it makes me wonder. I remember when I was reading *Uncle Tom's Cabin,* there was a runaway slave who had the initial of his master's last name burned in his hand. It seems to me I've read where they did it for other reasons, but I can't remember."

Manfred raised his eyebrows and took in a breath. "Oh, they used to brand felons when they brought 'em over here from England. Called it transporting them. They burned 'em in the hand so they couldn't go back to England. But that was a hundred-fifty, two hundred years ago. If you read *Moll Flanders,* you'll see it there."

"All I read by him was *Robinson Crusoe.*"

He went on. "As far as I know, it's not a common practice anywhere nowadays. Even *Uncle Tom's Cabin* was written some forty years ago, and nobody's got slaves to brand any more. And I'd warrant this fella's no—" Manfred paused with the rolling pin in his hand and a thoughtful expression on his face. "You never know," he said. "There's still pirates and other types of thugs, especially in the dark parts of the world, who take people captive and mark 'em in some way. You don't know where-all some men have traveled. This fella seems like he's been around."

"He does. I wonder where he's from, where he came from."

Manfred rolled out the smaller ball of dough. "For all I know, he came from Ultima Thule, and plans to go back."

"Where's that?"

Manfred laughed. "In ancient times, it was the farthest point north that anyone knew of. Where people go around wrapped in furs." He laughed again. "Sorry. I had the idea of this fella coming down from there, with ice on his mustache, getting burned in his hand, and then going back to stick his hand in the snow for a couple of centuries."

I must have given him a quizzical look, because he went on to apologize again.

"Sorry. I read too many books. I ought to take up whittling."

I shrugged. "It's an interesting idea, some place in the distant north. Where do you come across things like that?"

"Longfellow, as I recall." He rolled the dough crosswise to his earlier movements.

"Uh-huh." I could picture the volumes on my father's bookshelf. I had read *Evangeline* and the other schoolroom poems, but there was a great deal I had ignored. I said, "Nothing wrong with reading books, I hope."

"Not in my view. Some people burn 'em, you know."

"Oh, yeah." Ruth had told me about Tut burning a couple of books that one of her earlier admirers had given her. I followed that thought back to the tall fellow I had seen in the saloon. "So," I said, "you think Tut Whipple might have brought in some kind of a bully?"

Manfred took up the empty can, and as he cut out four more biscuits he said, "I don't know, but it's something he could do. He's not the type to let go easy. You know that."

"Sure."

"He's an opportunist, and he looks out for his own interests." The cook scattered flour across the top of all the raw biscuits. "You've heard of the idea that rain follows the plow."

"I think so."

Manfred went on to explain anyway. "It's the idea that once people plow up an area and plant crops, it'll attract rain. People actually believe it. It probably happened in a place or two, by coincidence, and they derived this religious-like idea out of it."

I nodded, waiting to see where he was going to take the idea.

He paused with a calm expression on his long face. His graying hair and Vandyke beard made me think he could have been like Longfellow or Whittier. A thinker, at least.

"Well," he said, "your friend Whipple follows the plow, in a manner of speaking. Not like rain clouds but like crows or gulls. Have you seen 'em? They follow a plow through the field to see what kinds of worms and grubs it turns up. That's Whipple. He follows the idea once it's been laid out—he's not a planner or a visionary on his own—and he looks out for whatever he can get for himself. Someone stands in his way, and he'll fight for it."

"I can believe that," I said. As for his comparison with the crow, it reminded me of Dunbar, looking to see what he could turn up. But the comparison went only so far. My sense of Dunbar was that he was not a follower or an opportunist. He was turning the ground himself, while Whipple was busy covering it up. But then again, if he was following Whipple . . . I shook my head to keep from thinking in circles.

Manfred was laying the raw biscuits in the oven tray and humming his tune about potato soup. "Where did you hear that song you told me about?" he asked.

"In the Castle."

"Oh, well, you made the rounds. Did you get to see your girl?"

"She's not exactly my girl."

He pushed out his lower lip. "That's all right. It's none of my business anyway. Just something to talk about."

"Well, to answer your question, I didn't get to see her."

He stooped and squinted as he opened the oven. "Too bad. But you're young. Rome wasn't burned in a day." He closed the oven door and stood up. "You look like you've got a question."

"I don't think I've ever seen those gulls you mentioned."

"Oh, they're like seagulls, mainly white, but they've made their way inland. They hang around garbage dumps, and they follow plows in the field. Shriek a lot, like sea birds. They're a nuisance."

"I can imagine."

"It's not important anyway. It doesn't put grub on the table. Why don't you bring in some firewood?"

I could see he was getting down to the business of serving the evening meal, so I did as he asked. As I was finishing, Rumsey and Odell came in. They were both damp around the edges where they had washed up, and they relaxed in their chairs as they waited for supper.

Rumsey spoke in his good-natured tone as he asked, "Where's Hig?"

"He went over east to talk to a couple of others about the roundup," said Manfred. "I don't expect him back until tomorrow."

Rumsey pursed his lips and tipped his head. "Just seems kinda empty. Where's Dunbar?"

"He's off on his own, about like usual," said the cook.

Odell's cheekbones looked burnished after a day in the sun and then a splash of water, and his light brown eyes had a hard stare. "He gets around, doesn't he?"

"What do you mean?" I asked.

"Oh, he just seems to me like some kind of a range detective, and I don't know if he's here to check on us or someone else."

Manfred set a pot of beans on the table. I could see squares of bacon rind floating on the top.

"I don't think he is," said the cook. "I don't think Hig would hire someone and bring him in like that without telling the rest of us. He just doesn't do things that way."

Odell's brow tensed. "Not that we know, anyhow."

Rumsey gave a light shrug. "I don't see where Dunbar's doin' any harm, but I admit I don't know if he's up to somethin'." He looked at the cook. "What do you think?"

"You want to know?"

"Sure."

Odell and I both nodded.

"I think Dunbar's looking for something on his own, and Hig's letting him do it, with the hopes that it might upset the water project."

"That's what it seems to me, too," I said. Now I had a picture of Dunbar turning up the ground as Hig followed and watched. Then I added, "But if I thought of it, it must be pretty obvious."

"I don't trust him all the way, though," said Odell.

"Grey knows him better," said Rumsey. "And he was with him the day he thumped Stiver. That's worth somethin'." He ladled himself a serving of beans.

"I'm like Grey," said Manfred. "I thought it was almost too obvious."

"So you think he's on no one's side but his own," said Odell, his voice in a grumble.

Manfred's tone was conceding as he said, "I don't know." After a second he went on to say, "But he doesn't seem like the selfish type to me. On the other hand, I don't think he's working for anyone else—at least not for anyone around here, in the way you suggested." He motioned with his head for Odell to serve himself, and then he added, "But we'll probably all get a chance to judge for ourselves."

Chapter Seven

Higgins rolled a thin cigarette and lit it. He turned his head a quarter turn to put his squinty brown eyes on Dunbar, who sat on his right.

Dunbar's face gleamed and his hair was combed, as he always came to the supper table neat and clean. He returned Hig's gaze with an open expression as he reported on what he had seen over by the Rim.

"They've laid out about a mile of ditch. They made a couple of passes lengthwise and didn't do much more than scratch the land, but now he's got two teams goin' back and forth crossways and scrapin' it out. It'll be a while until they actually cut off the range, but if we wait until roundup to get the cattle out of there, we might trample some ditch banks and give cause for someone to complain."

Hig shook his head. "We don't need that. I don't like to give up that bit of range, seein' as it's public domain, but it's not enough to get into a fight about. How many head do you think are there?"

Dunbar's eyes were clear and steady. "I'd say about twenty-five pair, and maybe another thirty at most of yearlings, two-year-olds, and the like."

Hig wrinkled his nose. "That's a few more than I thought."

"I might be off."

"It doesn't matter. They can't stay there anyway, so it's just a matter of pushin' 'em over this way sooner than we planned."

"That's what I figured."

"Make it harder for 'em to help themselves to our beef, too."

"I would guess they've laid off that for the time bein'."

Hig nodded, and his eyes closed a little more as he took a drag on his cigarette.

Without thinking, I let my eyes wander, and at that moment I saw Odell giving a hard stare at Dunbar. I wouldn't have called it jealousy, but maybe resentment. After all, here was Dunbar talking to the boss almost as an equal while the other hands were being ignored.

"Here's what I think," said Hig, still talking to Dunbar. "The four of you go over there together in the morning, and you push all the Little Six cattle back this way about three or four miles, maybe a little further. Don't bust your ass for somethin' that doesn't have our brand, but don't bother to cut it out, either. Everything's got to come out of there in another month anyway. Just don't put a rope on anything that hasn't got the Little Six brand on it, you know that." Hig looked around at the rest of us. "You boys hear that all right?"

We all nodded and said, "Sure." I could tell, though, that Odell was nursing some small grudge. I couldn't tell whether he didn't like Hig talking to Dunbar as if he was a kind of foreman or whether he was still suspicious of whose side Dunbar was on. But if Hig said the four of us were going out to gather and move cattle in the morning, that was what we were going to do.

We rode out of the Little Six ranch yard as the sun came up. It was a fresh morning, just cool enough to remind a fellow that summer was moving along and the colder weather was not far away. All four of us were wearing jackets and leather riding gloves, and each of us had a slicker tied to the back of the saddle.

At first we rode like an orderly quartet, with Dunbar's blue roan about a neck ahead of my sorrel, then Rumsey and Odell behind us in a similar pair. After a while, though, Odell let his horse out and took off ahead of the rest of us. He was riding a long-legged bay, and I imagined the horse was restless, but it also occurred to me that Odell might have been getting out ahead just to show that he didn't have to stay in line behind Dunbar. So the bay kicked up dust for half a mile until Odell slowed him down and walked him in a circle.

When we caught up, Odell fell in alongside on my right. After that we did not ride in formation. Rumsey moved around to Dunbar's left, but his horse and mine had slower gaits than the other two, so from time to time, one of us would have to spur to catch up. Every once in a while Odell would lope his horse ahead of the rest and slow down to wait. And so we made our way across the prairie to the bluffs in the west.

The sun was warm at our backs by the time we came to the long scratch in the earth that marked the route of the ditch. We rode across it with no comment, but I saw each of the others do as I did—lift and turn his head to follow the line northwest through the grass and sagebrush.

On the other side, we found the first of the Little Six cattle. Three cows and two calves took off at a jiggling trot toward the bluffs, and Odell bolted out ahead and crossed in front of us. Rumsey kicked his horse and followed. The two of them circled around from the southwest and headed off the fugitives. They chased the cattle back our way, and when the animals had crossed the ditch line, Odell turned the bay horse and came to meet Dunbar and me.

"Gene and I'll go into the canyon and get any others," he said. "You-all can keep pushin' 'em over that-away."

If there was any challenge in the way Odell acted and spoke, Dunbar did not rise to it. Instead, he said, "Sooner or later, we'll have to work these bluffs to the south as well as the north."

I could see what Dunbar meant, that it would be better to start on one end, probably the south, and work to the other, rather than start in the middle. But Odell reined his horse toward the bluff and said, "We'll get 'em," and he was off again.

Once we settled into the method, it was not a bad way to get the cattle out and headed across the country. The more we moved along, the more the ditch route seemed like a dead line, and I didn't like crossing it. When I looked at it lengthwise, though, it just looked like a long scratch on the body of the land.

We had pushed out about twenty head when Odell and Rumsey called for a noon break. The four of us got down from our horses and sat in a small pow-wow circle right there on the open plain. We had all taken off our jackets by then, and the overhead sun warmed the ground while a breeze from the east carried the scent of sage and dry grass to mix with the smell of warm horses. It was a peaceful setting, but I could see that Odell was irritable.

"I don't like any of this," he said. "Until someone puts up a fence, there'll be no end of crossin' and re-crossin' this ditch. How much water do they plan to run down this thing, anyway?"

"I've got no idea," said Dunbar. "But you can bet it'll be enough for cows to get stuck in it and drown."

Odell tore at the grass in front of him. "They should just leave the country the way it is."

Dunbar shrugged. "If they did that, no one could be here. Not that I like some of it, but if people want to make a livin' off the land, it's going' to get cut up, whether it's by roads, railroads, fences, or ditches. I haven't seen enough ditches to know for sure, but up until now, the railroads have been the worst. But they're the ones that made the cattle business possible. You can't walk these steers all the way to New York and Boston, or even Chicago."

"I know that," Odell grumbled. "But they ought to leave well enough alone."

"Oh, I agree," Dunbar answered. "Like I said, I don't like it. But people want progress, and they're gonna do it in a lot of different ways. This is small potatoes compared to what you'll see in a city."

"That's why I don't go there."

I was waiting to hear Dunbar's answer when the sound of horse hooves made us all look up. Two riders were coming at a fast walk from the direction of the reservoir and work camp.

The one on the left I recognized as Ingraham, Tut Whipple's lackey. I knew him by his short-brimmed hat with the low crown and by his cuffed trousers. He was riding a drab brown horse, one that I remembered from Whipple's stock, and he was using a saddle with wide stirrups that allowed his round-toed work books to stick through. He had his usual harmless look on his face, but I was sure he saw right away that Dunbar was with us, and I remembered his wide stare when Dunbar had taken care of Stiver.

It took me a few seconds to place the other rider. He was a tall man riding a sand-colored horse of Whipple's. He wore a tan, tall-crowned hat with four dents in the peak, and he had long stovepipe boots with his pants tucked in. The hat and boots gave him an elongated appearance as he sat in the saddle, and even though I did not recall either of those features from before, I recognized him as the tall duck who had been with Tut Whipple in the Whitepaw Saloon.

The two men rode closer and did not dismount when they stopped within a few yards of us.

"Afternoon," said Odell as he raised his head and squinted.

"Same to you," answered the tall man.

I could see the tan stitching on his brown wool vest, plus red and blue beads on the cuffs of his gauntlets. It was evident that he took some pride in his appearance. He had straight brown hair, trimmed even, and a full brown mustache cut so that it looked like the end of a bristle brush. He hadn't shaved for a couple of days, though, and the stubble made him look a bit porcine, as he had a chin that was not quite as firm as it should be and he had the makings of a second chin getting started below it.

"What can we help you with?" asked Dunbar.

"Name's Falke. George Falke. I work for Mr. Whipple. Maybe you know Mr. Ingraham here."

Dunbar nodded in that direction. "I've met him."

"And your name?"

"Dunbar."

Falke's muddy brown eyes roved across the rest of us and came back to Dunbar. "You all ride for the same outfit?"

"That's right." Dunbar's dark eyes were calm and steady as he answered.

"Well, I came to tell you that Mr. Whipple doesn't like your animals runnin' back and forth across our work."

Odell spoke up. "It's like we told Stiver. You don't like it, put up a fence."

"I'm not talkin' to you." The muddy eyes had flickered to Odell and now came back to Dunbar. "What do you have to say?"

"I don't have anything to add."

"Why are you runnin' cattle across our work, then?"

Odell piped up again. "For your information, we're clearin' 'em out of here."

"Keep out of this, sonny. I'm talkin' to this chap." With his eyelids relaxed, Falke gazed at Dunbar and said, "What about it?"

"It's just like he told you. We're moving the cattle back over our way."

"They're just gonna drift back here, and I'm tellin' you Mr. Whipple doesn't like it."

"I don't expect him to. And I'm not surprised he sent someone to tell us."

"What's that supposed to mean?"

Dunbar frowned. "It means I'm not surprised. What else do you want?"

"I want you to give me a straight answer."

"I'd say you got one."

Falke turned to Ingraham and said, "Get down." Then he swung down from the sand-colored horse and handed his reins to Ingraham.

Dunbar, meanwhile, pushed himself to his feet, as did the rest of us. Dunbar kept his eyes on Falke and said, "It would have been better manners if you'd gotten down from your horse to begin with. You're kind of a tub, aren't you?"

Falke did have some extra weight pushing out around the bottom of his vest, but he did not show any response to the comment. He drew his right hand back and rested it on his hip, not far from the butt of his six-gun. "Have it your way," he said.

"Fists." Dunbar handed me his hat and then his gunbelt.

Falke did not take off his tall-crowned hat, his beaded gauntlets, or his gunbelt. He moved forward in all his bulk and swung out his hand as if he was going to cuff a kid.

Dunbar did not humor him. He punched Falke square in the face, and the big man pulled his head back and opened his mouth. Beneath the bristle brush of a mustache, blood appeared on the man's large teeth.

Dunbar stepped in and gave him two more hard, quick ones that turned the man's head each way and sent the tall-crowned hat tumbling backward. Then he punched Falke in the midriff and slugged him one more time in the jaw.

Falke landed like a burlap sack of grain, heavy and shifting, and brought his right hand up his thigh toward his holster.

"Don't try it," said Dunbar. His hair was unruffled, and his charcoal-colored vest was still buttoned and in place.

Falke rolled over onto all fours, and with his back to Dunbar he reached for his hat. He put it on as he rose to his feet. He still did not turn to face Dunbar but reached toward Ingraham and took the reins. He turned the sand-colored horse and began to lead it away.

Dunbar looked at Ingraham. "Tell your boss we got his message."

Ingraham did a good job of not looking at anything or anyone in particular as he nodded and then turned to follow the other man and horse.

I was glad when I had the next opportunity to go into town, as I was on my own once again. It was a sunny day with a mild breeze from the east, and my horse covered the ground at a good pace. I rode in on the west side of the pond, crossing the plank bridge and then letting my horse take the slope at a run. It had been a week since my last visit to town, and as I had not seen Ruth on that trip, I thought I would drop in on her first. The day was still balmy, and I felt light-hearted as my horse took me up the hill. My spirits sank, though, when I saw Dunbar's buckskin tied to the hitching rail in front of Whipple's house.

The afternoon shade had begun to creep out from the house, and the two people sat in plain view in the soft shadow.

I couldn't imagine riding on without stopping, especially when they each raised a hand in greeting, so I turned into the yard and dismounted. Dunbar and Ruth were seated about a yard apart in cane-back chairs that I knew well. Dunbar sat with his hat on his knee, and his dark head made a contrast with Ruth's light hair, which was gathered in back but not tied up in a bun. In a more subtle match, his charcoal-colored vest was a few shades darker than her gray dress. I thought they looked relaxed, comfortable in one another's company, but proper all the same.

"Hello, sport," said Dunbar. "Takin' the air?"

"Good afternoon, Grey," came Ruth's cheery voice.

I stood with my reins in my hands as I looked from him to her. "I'm on my regular trip," I said. "I didn't mean to—"

"Not at all," he cut in. "I just got here myself. I should probably move on and let you do your visiting."

"Oh, no," I said. "I wouldn't have stopped if I hadn't seen someone outside."

Ruth's voice came up in a playful tone. "Don't say that. I would have ways of knowing if you rode by without stopping."

I was helpless when she spoke that way. I couldn't fudge, and I couldn't try to take the upper hand. So I stood there flat-footed and mute. Meanwhile, Dunbar showed no intention of moving on, in spite of what he had said.

Ruth spoke again, her voice still airy. "I think it's been a couple of weeks since you've dropped by, Grey. Hasn't it?"

"Something like that." I still felt as if something in the earth was pulling my spirits down.

"Well, don't be in such a hurry." She glanced at Dunbar and brought her eyes back to meet mine. "There's nothing confidential here, certainly nothing to exclude a friend." Her eyes tightened as she made a smile.

"Even at that, I can drop by on my way back. I've got a couple of errands to do, and I really should tend to them first." I pulled my reins through my hand.

"There you go," she said, lighter now. "And I won't ask what kinds of errands."

"Nothing confidential," I replied, and a smile came to me. I knew that in the motherly part of her fondness for me, she didn't approve of my going to saloons, and in the boyish part of my affection for her I didn't mind letting her worry like a mother once in a while. I touched my hat and said, "I'll see you later," but I didn't say when. Then I nodded to Dunbar.

"We'll see you, Grey. Don't worry."

I didn't know what I would worry about, but I nodded again as I turned toward my horse. I did not look back as I mounted up and rode away.

I had a lasting image of the two of them sitting there. The scene had a distinct quality—a tone, perhaps—that told me they had gotten to know each other on their own since the day I introduced them. On that earlier occasion I thought Dunbar had sidled up to get information or impressions for his own purposes, whatever they were, but the tenor of this recent scene was that things had progressed.

There was no denying to myself that I resented his familiarity with her, and I was chafed at her as well. I also knew it was not a matter of moral indignation on my part. I was truthful to myself on that score and had been for as long as I had loved Ruth. I really didn't think it was doing Tut Whipple any wrong, because he himself did not see anyone else's attentions as being worth his worry. I was convinced that he did not value his wife's commitment to him in and for itself, but rather as a proof of his mastery; and as long as he had control, anyone else's efforts were as serious to him as dirt clods flung at a stone wall.

So I was not offended by the *tête-à-tête*. I was just jealous, and it took some effort to remind myself of what my father would have told me: it was none of my business, and life would be easier if I dwelt on things I could do something about.

With that thought, I rode past my father's office, past the Whitepaw Saloon and the blacksmith shop and the rising stone walls of the bank, until I came to the last building on the way out of town. Outside the roadhouse, two cow ponies stood tied to the hitching rail. I headed that way, but before I came to a stop I saw a figure step into the open from the other side of the building.

It was Rachel carrying a bucket on her way to the cistern. First, I recognized her dark shiny hair and shapely figure, and then I saw her face, bronze in the sunlight. She waved at me, and I waved back. I appreciated her simple grace as she set the bucket on the cover of the cistern and moved a board aside.

I rode to the end of the hitching rail and dismounted. She had hooked the bucket to the rope and now let it down with the windlass.

"Nice to see you today," I said.

She brushed a few loose hairs away from her cheek as she turned at the waist. Her dark eyes sparkled, and she smiled. "It's been a little while. Where have you been?"

"Oh, here and there. I dropped by the last time I was in town, but I didn't find you."

She smiled. "I'm almost always here."

"Well, it doesn't matter. I get to see you now."

She turned the handle and brought up the dripping bucket, which she sat on the board cover. "Are you going to come in?"

"Oh, I don't know. It would just be to see you. I'm not hungry." I hesitated. "You're probably busy anyway."

She winced a little. "I have to take this water to the kitchen, and then I have to wash the dishes and clean everything."

"I could carry the bucket for you."

She glanced toward the rear of the building. "I think I'd better do it myself."

I could almost hear her mother's voice. "Sure," I said. "I'll drop by again before long."

"That's fine." The breeze waved her hair, and she brushed it again from her cheek.

I slapped the loose ends of my reins in my palm. "Good to

see you, then."

"And you, too." She lifted the bucket, leaving a dark ring on the dry lumber, and waved as she walked away.

I smiled though she wasn't looking. She had a light, carefree way about her as she carried the bucket of water, and it didn't throw her off stride a bit. Then I turned away in case she looked back, and I led the horse out a few steps. I looped the reins around the horse's neck and paused for a second with my toe in the stirrup. The melody of a song came drifting from inside the tavern, and I felt a bit of longing. Then I had a fleeting image of my last view of Rachel, and I was glad I hadn't gone past the moment.

As I rode toward the main part of town, past the grain warehouse with a hundred sacks of dead weight lining an interior wall, then the blacksmith shop with the fire bell in front, I saw the sun reflecting on the surface of the pond. After a few more steps the livery stable closed off my view, and I was in the center of town. I dismounted, tied up in front of the mercantile, and went in. Fenn Fuller's clerk was engaged in conversation with Ben Marston's man Brownie, who leaned forward in heavy-browed, thick-lidded attention. Fuller's clerk saw me and went to the postal window. As was the case more often than not, there was no mail for the Little Six. Not seeing Fenn in the store, I went out and crossed the street to the Whitepaw Saloon.

Fenn Fuller was sitting in his usual place, with his hat on the post behind him. He raised a hand in greeting and waved me over. The only other person at the table was Al Redington. I had just seen Henry Dornick at work, where the sun glinted on that singular dust that settles on men who work with cement and mortar, so I did not expect to see him in the shady interior of the saloon. Lon Buckley was tending the bar, where three riders each had a spurred boot lifted onto the brass rail. A quick glance up and around assured me that the bobcat and the Indian warrior were still holding their places.

I sat down so that I formed a triangle with Fuller and Redington. Lon brought me a glass of beer, said good afternoon, and went back to his post.

"Well, boy," said Fenn Fuller in his best attempt at being comradely. "What's new?"

"Not much that I know."

He gave a small laugh. "It's a rare man who can say he really knows something. Everyone says, 'The older I get, the less I know.' "

Redington finished taking a drink of beer and set down his glass. "Isn't that the truth?"

"It's just that you realize it more as you get older," Fenn went on. "That's why they say, hire a sixteen-year-old while they still know everything."

"They don't know anything," said the butcher.

Fenn Fuller laughed again. "Of course they don't. They just don't realize it." He rotated his brandy glass, then looked at me through his spectacles. "I hear your fellow Dunbar had the opportunity to meet Whipple's new man."

"It was a brief exchange."

"Ha-ha. That's what I heard. Big fella hit the dirt right away."

"Dunbar's no shorty," I said. "He's got a pretty good reach. I've seen it twice now."

"I suppose." Fenn arched his eyebrows. "Maybe his reach will get him in trouble after all."

I frowned. "I'm not sure how you mean that."

"He gets around," said Redington. "Maybe it'll catch up with him."

I recalled the image of Dunbar and Ruth sitting in the shade, and even though I had been miffed at the time, I resented the butcher's comments. At the same time, I enjoyed knowing why he had a grudge against Dunbar.

Fenn Fuller changed the subject. "Movin' into that time of year when the air gets heavy. Have you noticed it, Grey?"

"Oh, yeah. Grass goes to seed, weeds turn ripe. Sagebrush starts drooping with its little clusters."

"I've heard," he went on, "but I don't know if it's true, that in places where they back up a lot of water, they get more humidity. Stands to reason, but I'd think that in a big, wide open area, a reservoir here or there wouldn't be much in proportion."

"I doubt it," said Redington. "You get up by the Great Lakes, maybe, but that's like another country. This little reservoir Whipple's building wouldn't be a pimple on a gnat's ass."

"But it's a big thing here." Fenn gave a quick nod.

"Oh, sure it is. They've got a goodly amount of money tied up in it. If Ben Marston says 'frog,' Whipple jumps."

"That's not all bad," said the merchant.

Redington shrugged.

Fenn Fuller pursed his lips and spoke again. "You have a man of influence like that, someone who can get backing and who can get others to move on things, and you've got a chance to make bigger things happen."

I could tell he was coming around to his pet topic of why we should have a railroad. I took a drink of beer and let myself relax.

"Well," said Redington, "that's all good and fine. I just hope Whipple can handle this job at hand."

Fuller perked up. "Oh, why shouldn't he?"

"Organization. Management. Anyone you talk to, you hear the same thing. He's always behind as far as time goes, and he's always spent way ahead of himself."

Fuller's expression tightened. "Well, that's someone's fault, and it's not hard to fix. You get a payment schedule, and you don't release money until certain stages or phases are done. Then if a man's behind on work and ahead on spending, he tightens the screws and tries to bring those two things together."

"Sure," said Redington, wiping his mustache, "everyone knows that. But if a man goes bust in the middle of the job—"

Fenn gave his little laugh. "They usually finish it, get what money they can, and go bust then. Take down all their creditors with them."

The butcher scowled. "Yet he's got money to bring in a big galoot who can't cut the mustard."

I could hear my father saying "muster" in a tone of correction, but I kept to myself and took another drink of beer.

Fenn Fuller had a smug look as he gave a wag of the head. "It's not over yet." He lifted his brandy glass and took a small sip, then licked his lip. His ruddy cheeks and silvery-red side whiskers made him look as much like the old fox as ever.

As I rode back to the ranch, the melody of the song I had heard from outside the Castle kept running through my head.

Dum-da-da-dum-da-da-dum-da,
Dum-da-da-dum-da-da-dum.
Dum-da-da-dum-da-da-dum-da,
Da-dum-da-da-dum-da-da-dum.

After it had played through several times, I pieced in the words that I thought I had heard at some time in the past.

Meet me tonight in the moonlight,
Leave your little sister at home.
Meet me out back of the churchyard,
Don't leave me to wait all alone.

I sang that verse in a low voice as I rode across the shadowy grassland. The saddle leather squeaked and the air cooled, and every once in a while my horse threw his head and snorted. One song was like another to him.

Back at the ranch, I saw that Dunbar's buckskin had not returned to the corral or pasture. I supposed he was still off somewhere.

Everyone had something to do, it seemed. Whipple was busy putting up mounds of dirt, Dunbar was occupied with his own mysterious affairs, and the council was busy sorting through other people's business. The subject of Annie Mora hadn't come up when I was in the Whitepaw Saloon, but I remembered her now. I wondered where she was and whether she, too, was busy. I was impressed once again with how busy everyone was and how easily they had let her disappearance go unresolved. As I washed my face at the pump, I realized I was like the rest of them, as far as doing anything went. The difference was that even if I was able to do something, I wouldn't know where to start.

Chapter Eight

Dunbar saddled his blue roan while I did the same to a dark horse out of my string. I had been working at the ranch long enough that I knew my way around horses, and I had my own saddle, which had been my father's. I also had my own rifle and six-gun, and I knew how they worked, so I was no greenhorn. Still, I felt like a kid in the presence of Dunbar. As he went about rigging his horse, every move was smooth and flawless. Self-assurance emanated from him, as did a feeling of power from the blue roan. Dunbar grained his horses well and rode them often, so they were well muscled. He also kept horseshoes on them, while it was common with many outfits, Hig's included, to run the cow ponies unshod in grass country.

We led the horses out into the yard, and I waited for Dunbar to mount up. He had a light, effortless way of stepping into the stirrup and swinging his right leg over. Some men went at it laboriously, starting with a left hand on the saddle horn and a right hand on the cantle, then shifting the right hand and turning in the air. Others, mostly tall men it seemed to me, pulled themselves aboard with the right hand. I thought Dunbar's method was a good one. He started side-by-side with the horse and pulled himself up with his left hand on the saddle horn. He barely touched the pommel with his right hand, and I could tell he was used to keeping it free to hold a lead rope. He carried his rifle in a scabbard, but I imagined he had had plenty of practice mounting with one in his right hand.

On this day, we both had to swing a little higher to get on board, because we were packed to stay out overnight. It was Dunbar's idea, and Hig went along with it. For my own part, I wasn't very keen on Dunbar's company at the moment, but no one asked me. So with grub in our saddlebags and our bedrolls tied on, we rode out onto the prairie as the sun cleared the distant hills in the east.

The bluffs of Decker Rim showed in the distance where they began in the south, some twenty miles away, and ran to the northwest. All across Decker Basin, the morning sun cast shadows in the swells and gashes of the grassland. The fluting sound of a meadowlark lifted on the air, and horse hooves swished in the dry grass. I had cooled down from the first exertion of saddling my horse, and I was glad to be wearing a jacket. I tensed my upper arms and squeezed them against my sides, and the short flow of warmth made me yawn. Dunbar, half a length ahead, raised a gloved hand to shift the toothpick in his mouth. He did not say where we were going, but from the direction he had set, I assumed we were going a ways south of the place where we had met up with Ingraham and Falke a few days earlier.

We took it slow through the morning, poking here and there to look at brands but not pushing cattle in any direction. I had the impression that we were doing what Dunbar often did on his own. By late morning the day had grown warm and dry, with grass particles and dust rising from the horses' hooves. We were still a few miles from the bluffs, with no trees anywhere in sight on the grassland, so we sat in the shade of our horses when we took a rest.

Dunbar's eyes were narrowed as he gazed out across the range. "Every part of the country's got its own," he said. "Cattlemen and wheat farmers, they like this kind of country. Feel at home, even when the hard wind blows and never seems to stop.

Others, I guess, they can't handle the big wide open. It eats on 'em. They need to be closed in by mountains or trees or buildings. I've heard of people goin' crazy with the wind. Have you?"

"Just talk. I've never known of a particular case, especially around here."

"Down in the Southwest, they say people wander out into the desert and disappear. Never give a reason why, and no one ever finds 'em. Down there, you know, people use the buzzards to help find some pilgrim or sheepherder who got his brains baked and couldn't find his way. But these others, it's as if they wander out and don't want to be found."

"Could be," I said.

"Up on these northern plains," he went on, "people freeze to death." With a motion of the head, he waved his hatbrim toward the west. "Higher up, where the snow never melts, they might keep for a long time."

"I suppose."

"Well, like I say, every country's got its own. Have you ever eaten prairie dog?"

"No, and I hope I don't have to."

"Same with me. I've eaten jackrabbit more than once, and I hope I don't have to go any lower than that."

I didn't feel like being humored, so I didn't say anything.

After a minute, Dunbar spoke gain. "I guess some of the old-timers ate whatever they could find when they first came out this way. Prairie dog, jackrabbit, coyote."

"I like beef," I said.

"So do I. Problem is, so do a lot of others, and they don't always pay for what they eat."

"Is that what we're out looking for?" As soon as I said it, I wished I hadn't given in and asked.

"We're out lookin' for whatever we can see. But with a shortage of Spanish treasures and lost prospectors in this part of the country, we're more likely to find where someone's livin' off the fat of the land, in a place where the land doesn't have much fat of its own."

It seemed like a lot of work just to try to catch someone at butchering a head or two of range cattle, but I understood, or at least thought I understood, that any discoveries against Whipple and his crew might complicate things to someone else's satisfaction. And even if we didn't find evidence of any illegal handling, Whipple's caution might lead him to have to pay for all his beef, which in turn could make money scarcer for him. To use Fenn Fuller's figure of speech, I saw that more than one party could tighten the screws on Tut Whipple and make it more difficult for him to carry out the job.

Dunbar did not seem to take pleasure in the prospect, however. I didn't know if it was all matter-of-fact to him or whether Decker Basin was like one large chessboard and he was planning half a dozen moves in advance.

At midday he took us to a canyon where a faint trickle of water seeped out of the base of the sandstone and gathered in a tepid waterhole. From the way Dunbar directed his horse and dropped a word now and then, I guessed that he knew every cleft and canyon along these bluffs and visited them to look for new sign. Still, he was unhurried. We loosened our cinches, let the horses drink, and dug out some cold biscuits for lunch. After we had eaten, he said we could lay up for a while and let the horses rest.

The sun seemed not to move overhead, and the hot, still air in the canyon made me drowsy. I gave in and drifted to sleep.

I awoke at the sound of horses snuffling. Dunbar was sitting in a crouch, looking out onto the rangeland.

"I don't see anything," he said. "But it's probably time to be moving along anyway."

We worked in and out of the small canyons for the next few

hours. Each time we came out and paused in the open, I enjoyed the light breeze as it brushed my face. Only twice did we find Little Six cattle that had drifted back this far, and when we did, we drove them eastward for about three miles and then returned to our slow operation.

In the early evening, as shadows crept out from the canyon walls, Dunbar picked a spot for our camp. We had watered the horses at a scummy waterhole half an hour back, and I was hoping for a cool spring or creek. The canyon he picked for us had cedar and chokecherry trees, but no water.

"Are we dry camping?" I asked.

"That's right."

"I sort of like to camp by water."

"So do I, when there's plenty of it, like lots of spots along a stream. But just a spring or waterhole, there's no reason to keep the regular animals from comin' to get what's theirs."

We unsaddled our horses and picketed them where the ground broadened out in the mouth of the canyon.

"Cold camp, too?" I asked.

"It's just as well."

As we ate the cooked beef and cold biscuits that Manfred had sent along, I gazed eastward where the land spread away. The shadows had stretched out further, and the whole grassland was mottled with spots of darkness. Dunbar and I were sitting on our bedrolls with our saddles on the ground behind us. I felt as if we were two little spots under a big arching sky.

When Dunbar finished eating, he stood up and brushed the crumbs from the front of his shirt. Then he sat down again and unbuckled his spurs. He laid them on his bedroll and said, "Think I'll go up top and take a look around."

"You want me to go?"

"No, you can stay here and watch the camp. I don't expect to see anything in particular. It just that sometimes it's interesting to see how much is goin' on when you think everyone has called it quits for the day."

"Sure," I said. "I'll stay here and keep an eye out."

"Go ahead and relax. Roll out your blankets if you want."

I sat in the gathering dusk as his footsteps crunched away. I didn't move except to shift my feet, and after about half an hour I heard him come back. Night was falling, but I could still see the horses where they grazed on their picket ropes. Then I saw Dunbar, sauntering out of the gloom.

"See anything?" I asked.

"Nothing of note, but no harm done. It's like hunting or fishing. You don't get something every time you go out." He sat on the bedroll and buckled on his spurs again. Then he unstrapped the bundle and rolled it out.

I did the same, and we sat facing each other as we pulled off our boots.

Dunbar spoke in his casual way. "One thing about not camping near water. You don't get as many gnats and mosquitoes. 'Course, you don't think of 'em when they're not around."

No water, no fire, just sitting on the ground in the middle of nowhere. It seemed like a lot of bother to me, but I crawled under the blankets and said, "Good night."

"Good night to you, Grey. It's been a good day's work."

Other than chase a few head of cattle, I wondered what I had done that day that could be called work. I stared at the night sky for a few minutes and then closed my eyes. I could hear Dunbar's even breathing, and from a ways off I heard the shifting of horse hooves on the dry ground. The distant howl of a coyote came across the plain, and then the night subsided into darkness and rest.

Hig, Dunbar, and I sat around the table after Sunday breakfast. Rumsey and Odell were doing the pearl diving, and Manfred was cleaning his cast-iron skillets. Hig took a pull on his tight cigarette and squinted at the far wall. Then from one second to the next, his eyebrows went up and his eyes opened. He looked at Dunbar and said, "I don't believe it's rained since you came here."

"Not that I've seen," said Dunbar.

"Well, we'll be in for some before long. We usually get a spell of cold, damp weather at about the time we start beef roundup."

Dunbar shrugged. "I guess we enjoy the warm weather while we've got it."

"Them that can." Hig ran his finger inside his bandanna and against his neck.

"Oh, uh-huh. I guess the dust and the sage and the pollen get to some people."

"Them," said Hig. "But I was thinkin' of dead people."

Dunbar's eyes widened. "Oh, did someone around here die?"

"It was a couple of weeks ago. Fella down by Bear Crick, name of Hugh Callahan. They said there was nothin' wrong with him that anyone could see. Just laid down and died."

"That's too bad."

"For him. But it could happen to anybody. If one thing don't git you, another will. Some men dig their grave with their teeth, you know, and some do it with their pecker."

"With their teeth?" I said.

Hig turned his narrow eyes on me. "They eat too much." He took a drag on his thin cigarette. "I think that's what got Hugh." Then, without any signal to change the subject, he asked, "What are you boys doin' today?"

Dunbar sat up straight. "I was invited to a little fiesta with our Mexican friends, and I was gonna invite Grey to go along."

Hig made a fizzing sound. "You'd probably like that, huh, Grey?"

"First I've heard of it." I looked at Dunbar. "Did someone

else get baptized, or married?"

"I think it's just a little get-together."

"Well, I didn't know anything about it."

He must have heard a sulkiness in my tone, for he said, "I was going to mention it in the next minute or two. Do you want to go?"

"I guess so."

Hig made his fizzing sound again. "When I was your age, we just went to the whorehouse. Keeps you from gittin' married." The way he said it made marriage sound like tuberculosis. His old eyes had a bit of a spark as he turned to Dunbar and said, "Isn't that right?"

Dunbar tipped his head. "It's one way. There are others."

"Like—?"

With a droll look, Dunbar said, "Bein' a priest. Dyin'."

Hig laughed. "By God, I'm glad I didn't have to do it either of those ways. Aren't you?"

"So far."

Dunbar rode his buckskin, and I rode a brown horse. We made it into town at about noon, going in on the east side of the pond and then turning left along the main street. Except for the café, everything was closed, so the center of town lay quiet and empty.

We went a block further and turned to the right, where we could hear people singing in the church. They were singing the hymn about the river and the shore. On our left, straight west of the church, Ben Marston's house sat back from the corner with its semicircular drive and gleaming portico.

A short way further took us to the *colonia,* where the smell of smoke and roasting meat wafted on the air. Four or five children were running around and laughing, and the undertone of men's voices came from the spot where the smoke was rising.

As on the previous occasion, Dunbar brought out a package wrapped in brown paper, and he gave it to one of the women. She thanked him and called out to the children, who all came running.

I went with Dunbar to join the men. They were gathered around a fire pit where the carcass of a young lamb was spread-eagled on a spit. I knew it was lamb because of the size, the shape, and the smell. The spit was the kind that got a quarter turn every few minutes and was held in place with a steel pin that went from the frame to a wheel on the near end of the rod. At the moment, the carcass was tilted at a forty-five degree angle. The fat along the back was melting in little rivulets and splashing a drop at a time in the hot coals below. Wisps of dark smoke rose where the liquid burned on contact.

I like fires, and I like the smell of roasting meat. I wouldn't have gone out of my way to tell Hig, but the aroma of the lamb, lifted on the air by the dry heat of the coals, had a pleasurable effect. I didn't follow the conversation the men were having, and I didn't know what the women beneath the roofed shelter were saying, but the voices had a musical cadence, and the whole tone of the gathering was amiable.

When it came time to serve the meal, Mr. Mora and one of the men who worked for Tut Whipple put on padded leather gloves. They lifted the spit from the rack and set the cooked animal on a large cutting board. Then with a carving knife, Mr. Mora went about cutting off the meat in chunks and shreds.

The woman who had served me at the previous party served me now. She set before me a plate of meat, beans, and rice, with a stack of corn tortillas on the side, wrapped in cloth. I was seated at the end of a long table, on one side, hoping Rachel might come and sit for a moment.

On this day, the chance passed me by. Rachel's mother kept her in a circle of women, who ate with their plates on their laps.

From time to time one of the women would get up to tend to the men, but Rachel stayed put, along with a couple of other girls a little younger.

The only person who spoke to me was a boy about six or seven, who was walking around picking a leg bone. He stopped next to me and asked me a question. I frowned to show I didn't understand, and he said it again.

"¿Por qué estás tan triste?"

Now I got it. He was asking me why I was so sad. I smiled at him and said, *"No triste. No triste."*

He gave an uncertain smile and went on his way.

A little while later, Dunbar was ready to go. I went over to where the women sat, and taking off my hat, I thanked them. I caught Rachel's eye, nodded to her, and turned away. I paused to thank the men, who smiled and nodded. Some of them were smoking cigarettes by now, and I noticed a couple had rolled theirs out of corn husks. I wondered if there would be singing later on, and I wouldn't have minded staying longer, but I took Mr. Mora at his word when he rose to shake my hand and told me I was always welcome and could come again.

As we were riding away from the fiesta, Dunbar said, "I think we've got time to go past that tavern they call the Castle. You know the place, don't you?"

"Sure," I answered. Being out on the edge of town, it was open on Sundays. At first it struck me odd that Dunbar would want to go there, but then it occurred to me that he might have heard something from Mr. Mora or one of the other men and he wanted to follow up on it.

Dunbar made a click-click sound, and the buckskin picked up its feet. My horse fell in with it, and we got to the Castle in less than five minutes. As we tied up next to the horses at the hitch rail, I heard voices rise and fall inside.

We walked in from the bright sunlight to the dim interior.

Clark was tending the bar, where half a dozen patrons were scattered along. Only two of them did not turn around to see who had walked in, and as my eyes adjusted I could see that one of the two was Tut Whipple. He was leaning against the bar and had his head turned away from the door. It looked as if he was engaged in conversation with Ben Marston's man Brownie.

The man in the brown bowler hat and corduroy jacket flicked a dull glance our way and returned his attention to Whipple. Each of them had a mug of beer on the bar top, and Brownie reached across his chest to lay his fingers on the handle of his mug. He had a lethargic way about him whenever I saw him, and he looked even more so as he reached for his beer. He was slumped with his whole right forearm on the bar, and his bowler was set back to show his burr head. His face had a relaxed, disagreeable expression, which might have come from a few pints of beer. His eyelids drooped, and his thick lower lip fell forward to show his gapped teeth. Even on a good day, he did not cut a handsome figure. He had a sagging stomach and a sloppy belt line for someone his age, which was around thirty, and he had a heavy chest and thick upper body, with smooth, meaty hands sticking out of the sleeves of his jacket.

In spite of his slothful aspect, he kept his eyes fixed as he raised his mug and tipped it. I could tell he was making an effort to seem like a sharp customer to Whipple, and I wondered how he came by such a version of himself. I imagined it came from the gun he packed in the holster beneath his coat. In the couple of years he had been around town, I don't think anyone saw him as much more than a lout who had the easy job of looking after Marston's house when the boss was gone and acting like a bodyguard when the boss was home. It was well known that he slept night and day and didn't do much when he wasn't sleeping.

Dunbar and I took a table and waited for Clark to come

over. Brownie was in my field of vision, and I paid attention when he stood up straight and set his mug on the bar. I thought he might be preparing to do something, but he just turned and, leaning forward, walked flat-footed to the back door that led to the privy.

A few minutes later he came back with the same motion, plopping his shoes on the wooden floor. He tossed a glance our way again, and I had the feeling that he didn't care for our presence.

Whipple kept his voice low, but Brownie didn't bother. His voice came out loud and flat, in an accent that I couldn't place but had heard before. It seemed like Ohio or Illinois or somewhere in that part of the country. From Brownie's comments I gathered that the two of them were talking about railroad beds and cross-ties. Brownie called the ties "sleepers," which I had heard before but didn't connect for a minute.

Their conversation hit a lull, and Brownie finished off his beer. He thumped the empty mug on the bar top and called out, "Hey, let's have another one and a bowl of stew."

Clark moved toward him along the back of the bar and said, "We don't have any stew today."

"Oh, the hell you don't," said Brownie. "Give me a bowl. I'm hungry."

"I tell you, there isn't any. The kitchen isn't open on Sunday."

"That's a hell of a deal."

I could hear the slur in his voice now.

"It's just the way things are," said Clark. "No hot food on Sunday. There's cold grub, but it's take what you get."

"Are your Mexicans too good to work on Sunday?"

"They could be Chinamen or bohunks, and it would all be the same." Clark had both hands on the bar, and even though he was going soft in the face, he gave Brownie a hard stare. I rather appreciated him at the moment.

"Well, I don't want no cold biscuits," said Brownie, his voice still loud and flat. "What I'd like is a steak, but since I'm in here I was willin' to settle for a bowl of stew."

Clark took hold of the empty mug. "Do you want another beer?"

"I said I did."

As Clark turned away to fill the mug, Brownie cast a heavy-lidded glance at our table. "I don't like the way you two are looking at me."

I spoke too quick and I knew it. I said, "You're the one causing a scene."

His eyes narrowed, almost shut. "Don't shoot your mouth off with me."

"Leave the kid alone," said Whipple.

"I don't like his attitude."

"Leave him alone."

"Just a smart-aleck kid." Brownie stood up from leaning on the bar. He shifted his feet to steady himself from weaving, and he breathed with his mouth open.

"Don't bother with him," said Whipple. "Here's your beer."

Brownie took a couple of steps toward our table and forced his stare on me. "I know who you are," he said. "Don't think you're any better than you are."

I frowned. I didn't have any idea of what he meant by that.

"You're just a dollar-a-day cowhand, and no great shakes at that. You're white, but you nose around with the Mexicans."

Dunbar gave me a frown and a light shake of the head, so I didn't say anything.

Brownie turned to Dunbar. "What do you know about it?"

"About what?"

"About the smell of lard."

Dunbar had a sharp look in his eye, but his voice was calm as he said, "You ought to lay off while you've got a chance."

Brownie came forward a few more steps and loomed over Dunbar's elbow and shoulder. "I know who you are, too."

"You know a lot."

Brownie tipped back his head and looked down his nose. "You didn't answer my question, though. About what you know."

"Just back off, fella."

"Huh." Brownie made a motion as if he was going to tap Dunbar's shoulder with the back of his hand.

Dunbar came up and out of his chair before I knew it. He grabbed Brownie by the lapels of the corduroy coat and walked him backward until he jolted into the bar.

Brownie reached his hand up between Dunbar's wrists, in the direction of the shoulder holster.

Dunbar shook the man, banging him against the bar, and said, "Go for it if you want, but it'll be the last thing you ever do."

Brownie sagged as Dunbar released him and stood back.

From behind the bar, Clark said, "Tut, I think your friend has had enough to drink. Why don't you take him out of here?"

"That's all right," said Dunbar. "We'll leave." He motioned to me with his head, and I got up to go with him. I took a parting look at my beer.

"We'll remember this," said Tut.

Dunbar paused. "What of it?"

"We'll remember that you threatened to kill this man."

Dunbar leveled his gaze at Whipple. "I'll tell you, friend, I don't mince my words when someone wants to pull a gun on me. It saved us all some trouble."

Outside, I asked Dunbar, "Why didn't you let them leave? We could have finished our drink."

Dunbar shook his head. "He's just the type to be out here waitin' for us, and he's too drunk to shoot straight." Then with a nonchalant expression, he added, "I wouldn't want him to hit you by mistake."

Chapter Nine

As I crossed the plank bridge on the west side of the pond, I imagined that if Dunbar was sitting in the front yard with Ruth again, they would hear the hoofbeats. I glanced at the surface of the pond, saw the reflection of the overcast sky, and then let my horse out so he could take the hill on a run.

No one sat in front of the house. The yard was empty. With the gray sky and the cool air, I had the feeling that time was drawing short. On the northern plains, the weather moves into fall before the calendar does. The colder air from the north comes as a reminder that the sun goes down a minute or two earlier and that winter is not far away. The chokecherry leaves turn muted shades of red, the cottonwoods go yellow, leaf by leaf, and one morning a fellow looks out and sees Decker Rim powdered in snow. He puts on and takes off his jacket half a dozen times a day, and even on a warm afternoon, the temperature falls at sunset. A man on foot or horseback can feel the difference when he goes into a draw and comes out. Those details of color and chill and fragile warmth lived in the memory and were summoned up, not singly but in a blend, as I cleared the hill and felt the northern breeze on my face.

I rode into the yard and dismounted. I called out as I often did. "Hello-o! Anybody home?"

The front door opened, and the light-colored figure of Ruth appeared. She stepped forward into the filtered sunlight, her blond hair clean as always and tied back, her bluish-gray wool dress in tone with the weather.

"Well, good afternoon, Grey," she said. "I didn't know when you would come to see an old woman again."

"Maybe I should be a country doctor," I said. "Make the rounds, feel the pulse of the old and feeble."

"I thought you would be a lawyer."

I smiled. "Do old women need lawyers?"

Now her light laugh came. "Some do."

Neither of us spoke for a few seconds. I looked at the sky and said, "A little change in the air."

"Oh, yes. It'll be dreary soon enough." Her blue eyes rested on me. "You'll be out working on the range, won't you?"

"Sure, but things usually warm up after the first squall."

"Indian summer," she said. "But still, that first wet weather is dangerous. I had a friend in school whose sweetheart was killed when his horse slipped on a hillside in the September rain." She forced a smile. "I'm sorry. I shouldn't be saying things like that to you."

"It's all right. I'm always careful, you know."

"Of course you are, but chasing cattle is full of quick turns."

"That's true." I rubbed my horse on the jaw and turned back to her. "Even your country doctor who carries his satchel in a buggy takes a spill once in a while. Seems like I heard of one of those."

"Oh, I have, too. Let's not talk about that any more. I'm sorry I got us started on it." She put on another smile. "What else is there?"

I shrugged. "I don't know. Well, maybe one thing. Do you know this fellow named Brownie, who works for Ben Marston?"

"I know who he is, that's all. I haven't met him. Why do you ask?"

"I saw him talking to Tut, and he got belligerent with us. Brownie did."

"With *us?* You and someone?"

"Um, yeah. Me and Dunbar."

"Oh."

"It was a few days ago. We had just stopped into the tavern, and there was Tut, and it looked like he was having some kind of conversation with this fellow Brownie. He's not doing any side work for Tut, is he?"

Her face showed surprise. "I wouldn't know. As for Tut, he has deep talk with everyone, if it looks like there's any business possibility. You know that as well as I do."

"I've seen it. Tut didn't mention the incident to you, did he?"

"Oh, no. He rarely does. What happened, or is it fit for a lady's ears?"

I smiled. "I'll give you a gentle summary. The fellow was causing a scene because there wasn't any kitchen food on hand, and then he decided he didn't like the way we were looking at him. As if we could help it, with the noise he was making. Anyway, he got too close to Dunbar, who had to back him up a few paces. Tut seemed to take umbrage, as Manfred would say, and I was wondering how much it would matter to him."

"He doesn't like your friend Mr. Dunbar, that's for sure. But beyond that, I don't know a thing. Men have their business, you know."

"Oh, yeah."

Another brief silence hung in the air until she spoke. "And what about this Mr. Dunbar, then?"

I felt a tinge of my earlier resentment. "I don't know. What about him?"

"Well, what do you know about him?"

"Not much. You probably know him as well as I do."

"Don't be that way with me, Grey. You know I'm asking you because I trust you."

Trust me not to say anything to anyone else, I thought. But I softened to her request. "He doesn't talk about himself very much," I said. "I don't know where he's from or where he's been. As far as that goes, he seems to have been everywhere. He's mentioned Chicago a couple of times, but I don't think he's a Pinkerton man. Not that I would know, but Manfred doesn't think so, either."

"What does he want?"

"Who, Dunbar?" I thought he wanted Ruth, but I said, "I think he wants to prove something."

"And what would that be?"

"I don't know." My eyes met hers. "Do you have any idea of what he might want to prove, if he does?"

"Sometimes it seems as if he wants to prove he's superior to everyone else."

"Maybe that's it," I said. I felt guilty at helping her feel that way, for I knew I still resented her interest in him. When I said I thought he wanted to prove something, I meant it in a different way than she took it, but I didn't tell her that. On the other hand, I was telling her the straight truth when I said I didn't know what, if anything, he did want to prove.

She gave a brief shiver. "It's good you're wearing a jacket today."

"Would you like to wear it for a minute?"

"Oh, no. I can go in and get something if I need it."

I took a full breath and pulled the reins through my hand. "Well, I didn't expect to stay long. I just stopped in long enough to say hello and see if you were all right."

"I know you have other stops to make."

She could make me feel like a kid any time she wanted. "Just for that," I said, "I won't set foot in any saloons today."

"All the better to stay away from belligerent people." A playful expression had come back to her face, and her white, even teeth showed as she smiled. "Enjoy yourself, Grey. When you become a country doctor, you won't be able to. You'll spend all your time taking pulses, feeling foreheads, staying up late at night listening to your patients' troubles. I can see you now, a tired man of fifty, hoisting yourself into your carriage and making the long, lonely trip back to town in the dark. A cold night, and you gave your last dram of brandy to a patient."

"You've got it all figured out."

Her blue eyes flickered at me. "If I had anything figured out, I wouldn't be here. Wait—I said that too quickly." She looked away. "What I meant was, if I had a better understanding of things in general, of how people came to be in the situations they are in and of how people managed their lives, mine might not be the same. But then again, perhaps what one learns is that things are not likely to change. Maybe those are the people who sleep well at night—the ones who know not to kick against the traces." Her eyes came back to me. "You're the only one I can say this to, you know. It's as if I'm the one who took your dram of brandy."

"You're welcome to it, Ruth."

She patted my cheek and gave a gentle smile. "You're a good boy, Grey. Come and see an old lady again."

"I will." I straightened my reins, led my horse a couple of steps away, and mounted up. I turned in the saddle and tipped my hat to her. "See you soon," I said.

She waved and said, "Be careful."

Five of us sat in the cook shack after supper. Just two weeks earlier we had the doors open to cool off the place, and now we were glad to have the warmth kept in. Manfred poured coffee from the blackened pot, and the cups got passed down from Hig to me and from Rumsey to Odell. Hig had rolled a thin cigarette and was smoking it with a distant expression on his face. Rumsey in his yellow bandanna and leather wrist cuffs was smoking his own pill, as he called it, which he had rolled in his relaxed way. Odell, strung a bit tight as always, had his cigarette in the corner of his mouth and squinted at the smoke as he worked his thumbs on the lariat he was oiling. Manfred, with his high forehead, long face, and graying Vandyke beard, had put on a pair of reading glasses and tilted his head up to read the newspaper.

Except for hints of autumn in the air, it felt like earlier times, before Dunbar came. Where he was at the moment, I didn't know, except that he was off on his own and would come back when he was done. I had the sense that he, too, felt the time growing shorter, as roundup would be getting under way before long, and then he would follow the wagon like the rest of us.

"Here's a fellow," said Manfred, shaking the paper, "got rheumatism in one hip while he was working as night watchman on a big stone building they were putting up—probably something like Dornick is doing, but on the railway where they need to have someone look after it. Anyway, the cold settled in his joints, and he couldn't move that leg hardly at all, until he discovered he could walk backwards. He did that, and dragged the leg at first, but by and by he got so he could use the leg again, and now he's walking like usual."

"Walking backwards?" I asked.

"That's right. Did that for a while. Now he's walking normal again."

"I've had dreams like that," I said. "Not being able to walk forward, and laboring to walk backwards."

Manfred folded the page over. "Don't take a job as night watchman in a stone building."

"You can get it sleepin' on the ground," said Hig. "Age catches up with you."

"This one was a young fellow," said Manfred. "About the age of these boys."

"Well, there you go," said Hig. "No one's safe. The weather gets cold enough that the snakes den up and don't get in your bedroll any more, and then the rheumatiz creeps in. Wonder any of us is alive."

Manfred arched his eyebrows as he scanned the paper. "Somebody, somewhere, is dying at every minute of the day. At this very moment, in Chicago or New York, someone is strangling or shooting or stabbing someone else."

I thought he had been talking philosophy with Dunbar, and I gave him a curious look. He ignored me and went on.

"Others in the world are dying of consumption, malaria . . ."

"Yeah, yeah," said Odell.

"Just lending cheer," said Manfred. "Here in the bosom of happy brotherhood."

Rumsey tipped his ash in the sardine can and said, "I 'magine there's lots of people out there who are happy, too."

"Oh, to be sure," said Manfred. "Many a man returning home from work, to be met by pretty wife and lisping child."

"Where do you get this?" Hig asked.

"From the story papers."

Hig wrinkled his nose. "I think there's more truth in this fella that had to walk backwards."

"Could be," said Manfred. "But then again, maybe he just dreamed it, like Grey did."

"Rheumatism is real. I've seen it." Hig made a small spitting sound.

"I don't disagree," said Manfred, "but so is homicide, though I haven't seen it. As for the happy man with darling wife and child, I suppose it exists somewhere."

"Let me know if you ever see it."

Manfred gave a smile, as if he knew something that the rest of us didn't. "I will. But I'll probably have to go a ways from here."

★ ★ ★ ★ ★

When Manfred woke us in the morning, I saw that Dunbar had not come in during the night. I did not think he had been off strangling or smothering a victim, nor did I think he had a double life with a wife and child to check in on. Rather, I imagined him snug in his bedroll somewhere out on the dark prairie, having spent the evening blended into the landscape as he watched for odd doings.

At breakfast, Hig gave the other three of us our orders for the day. Four of the Little Six horses had been running loose since the end of spring roundup, and Hig wanted them back in the cavvy, or horse herd, for the fall roundup.

"Bring 'em in and put 'em in the corral. Clean 'em up and trim their feet. If we get another rider, they'll go in his string."

"How about Dunbar?" I asked.

"It looks like he's busy today."

"No, what I mean is, whether he's going to work on roundup."

Hig's narrow eyes settled on me. "He damn sure better. What do you think?"

"I don't know."

Manfred spoke up from pouring coffee in the cups. "As soon as you boys get done with the horses, I need you to pull out the chuck wagon and start getting it ready."

"It's in pretty good shape," said Odell. "Sittin' in the shed, it's just got a little dust on it, is all."

"Look it over," said Hig. "Grease the axles, look underneath and see if there's any weak spots."

"I need to get it stocked," said Manfred. "Maybe as soon as the boys come back, I can get Grey started on that."

I tensed for a second. That should be the wrangler's job, but he was coming with another outfit. I didn't look forward to the long hours of double-bagging all the coffee, rice, beans, flour, and sugar.

"That'll be fine," said Hig. "If Dunbar comes back, he can give the other two a hand with the horses."

I noticed that no one asked where Dunbar was, though I'm sure the others wondered. A week or so earlier, when Odell had asked, Hig merely said he was working on his own. No one bothered to ask after that.

We saddled our horses and rode south to the area where the loose horses had been seen last. They weren't wild, and they stayed together, but they had been grazing on their own for over two months, and I was glad I hadn't been sent out by myself to bring them in.

The sun came up in a blazing red ball, seemed to sit for a while on the horizon, paled as it made a quick short rise, and then continued in a slow climb. Little by little, its warmth came to the grassland of Decker Basin. I could smell fall in the air—a combination of drying vegetation, dust, and sage, all carried on a cool breeze with a trace of humidity. When the grasshoppers clicked and whirred away, they sounded different—slower, duller—than they did in the thinner air of midsummer.

Off to the south, across the yellowish-gray waves of open range, the sunlight reflected on the tan clay bluffs of the Rim. We went down into a swale, and when we came out we jumped a group of three antelope, which flashed their white rumps and headed to the southeast on a dead run. We rode further, noting cattle and their brands when we came close enough.

With the breeze at our backs we kept going south. The place we were headed lay on the other side of a muddy flat where the water collected in the spring and early summer but by this time of the season shrank to a dark waterhole in the middle. We rode across the thin, cracked mud and dismounted when we came to the dark gumbo around the hole. Rumsey and Odell rolled cigarettes and smoked them as we let our horses drink from the murky water.

Rumsey, crouching as he finished his smoke, pointed at the hoofprints of unshod horses and said, "Looks like the ones we came for are somewhere around here." He stood up and stepped on the butt of his cigarette.

The three of us tightened our cinches and mounted up. The horses stepped out at a fast walk as we left the waterhole and climbed the gentle slope. I expected the tan bluffs to come into view again in the south, but as we crested the rise in the ground, I was surprised to see two men on horses waiting for us.

Part of my surprise came from the pairing—two men in different shades and shapes of brown. Mounted on the sand-colored horse he had ridden before, Whipple's hired man Falke had drawn himself up to his full height. He was wearing his tan, tall-crowned hat with four dents in the peak, a tan shirt and brown vest, and tan trousers tucked into his black stovepipe boots. To complete his outfit, he wore his buckskin-yellow gauntlets with red and blue beads.

To his right and our left, Ben Marston's man Brownie sat on a sorrel horse that I thought I recognized as belonging to the livery stable. The man looked out of place, slumped as he was in the saddle and wearing a bowler hat that would be much more at home in a billiard parlor than out here on the range. The same went for the shoulder holster that bulged under the brown corduroy coat.

Falke's eyes traveled back and forth over the three of us as we brought our horses to a stop. I was on the left, Rumsey was in the middle, and Odell was on the right. "Mornin'," said Falke.

Rumsey and I each said, "Good morning," but Odell held his tongue. I thought he was being sullen, though I couldn't see his face from where I was. It did seem, however, that Falke's eyes stayed on him for a few seconds.

Then Odell spoke. "What do you need?"

Falke tossed his head. "I could just as well ask you boys that."

"We're out lookin' for horses," said Rumsey.

"Lose some?"

Odell answered. "Not exactly. They've been out grazin', and we came to bring 'em in."

Brownie's loud, flat voice came up. "What kind are they?"

"Cow horses," said Odell.

"I think he means their color or markings," said Falke.

"Maybe he does. But it shouldn't matter to him. They've all got the Little Six brand on 'em."

Brownie spoke again. "How many?"

"Four," said Rumsey. "They usually graze together."

Falke's bristly mustache went up and down. Then he said, "Should've sent four men."

None of us spoke. I thought he was fishing for something that would give him a hint of Dunbar's whereabouts, and I wondered if the two of them had been sent out to brace him.

Falke's horse shifted, and mine did, too. Brownie kept his eye on me, which I didn't care for, but I tried to ignore him.

Now Odell spoke. "You didn't answer my question earlier."

"What's that?" said Falke.

"I asked you what you need."

Falke raised his chin and began to take off his gauntlets. He gave a matter-of-fact look downward as he tucked them in front of him, behind the swells of his saddle. Then he looked up and said, "Not so much a matter of what I need, or even what I want. Just tryin' to get back somethin' that turned up missin'."

"What did you lose?"

"I wouldn't say I lost it as much as someone took it."

"Then it's not out here wanderin' on its own."

"Oh, no. It's tied up."

Odell heaved a breath. "Well, we don't have time for guessin' games. So if you don't mind . . ." Odell relaxed and let slack in his reins.

"Actually, I do," said Falke, turning his horse to block Odell. "What I'm lookin' for is a lariat that disappeared on me."

A hardness settled on Odell's face. "I don't like the way you said that."

"I wouldn't expect you to."

"I know what you're trying to say, so why don't you come out and say it in plain words, in front of these others."

Falke's mustache raised as he gave a taunting smile. "Sure. I'll put it in plain words. Someone stole a good lariat from me, and it's just like the one you've got tied to your saddle."

Odell frowned. "What the hell makes you think this is yours? I've had it since before I came to this ranch." He waved his arm. "Ask either of these fellas, or anyone else at the Little Six." He heaved out a breath. "You're way out of line, mister."

"That's for me to decide." Falke nudged his horse forward and looked down at Odell's lariat. The sand-colored horse took another step, and Falke reached out his hand. "Give it to me for a minute," he said, "and I'll show you."

Odell glared at him. "I'll do no such a thing."

"Give it here."

"Get back."

"I don't want to have to take it from you." Falke leaned as if he was going to do just that.

"Don't touch it," said Odell, moving his horse to the side. "You don't touch another man's horse, or his rope, or his—"

Falke crowded toward him. "I said give it—"

Odell was turned in the saddle as he tried to pull his gun, and he was way too slow. Falke had his own gun out in a second, and he shot Odell through the midsection at a distance of six feet.

The scene burst into a melee of horses lurching, bucking, grunting, and squealing. By the time I got my horse under control, Odell's was running away and still kicking up its hind legs. Odell was on the ground, writhing. Falke was still sitting in the saddle with his gun drawn. He looked from Odell to Brownie, who had also hit the dirt and now came up hatless with a .45 in his hand.

Rumsey got his horse turned around, and he and I dismounted at the same time to see what we could do for Odell.

I looked up at Falke. If he was going to shoot me, he was going to have to do it in cold blood, because my gun was in my saddlebag. Rumsey was wearing his, but he showed no awareness of it.

We knelt by Odell, and his shirt and jacket were wet with blood. The ground beneath him was dark as well.

"Tim, are you any good?" asked Rumsey.

Odell moved his head back and forth. His hat had fallen away, and his blond hair reflected the sunlight.

Rumsey tried again. "Do you think you can ride if I catch your horse?"

Odell shook his head like before. He pushed out his lip with his tongue and said, "Son of a bitch shot me for nothing."

The sand-colored horse moved back, but I did not look up.

"Can we do anything for you, Tim?" I asked.

"Don't let him have it," Odell rasped. "It's not his."

I looked up to see if Falke was going after Odell's horse, but he was trotting toward Brownie's. I watched as he grabbed the reins, turned the horse, and brought it back. Brownie had retrieved his hat and put it on. Falke leaned in the saddle and held the other horse by the headstall as Brownie climbed aboard. Then the two of them rode north, in the direction of Winsome.

Chapter Ten

On the morning after we buried Tim Odell, Hig laid out our work for the next couple of days.

"Grey," he said, "you ride with Dunbar. He'll tell you if there's anything that needs to be done."

I nodded and turned to Dunbar. The expression on his face didn't give me much to go on.

Hig motioned with his head toward Rumsey. "Me an' Gene'll go out and git those four horses, and damn anyone who gets in the way."

"You'd think they had enough for the time bein'," said Dunbar. "But then again, you might have thought it before, and they just came back for more. And got it."

"Damn deliberate."

"Looks like it. Not much question but what Falke's carryin' out orders. I'm just surprised he takes Brownie along with him."

"Huh," said Hig, pinching the stub of his thin cigarette as he held it to his lips. "The way I heard it, Brownie's not invited as much as he invites himself."

"Really?" said Dunbar. He paused with his coffee cup halfway up from the table.

"It's just what I heard," said Higgins with a shrug. "Little birdie. Said the fella makes himself welcome out there and hangs around."

"Any reason why?"

Higgins pursed his lips. "The thought seems to be that he's

tryin' to learn what he can about Whipple's past."

Dunbar frowned. "What would he do that for?"

"I'd guess it would be to find out if Whipple pulled anything crooked in any of his earlier deals."

"A spy for the boss, then?"

"Somethin' like that." Hig didn't seem to mind it at all.

Dunbar pushed a toothpick at his lower teeth. "And here I thought Whipple was chummin' him up. Well, I think Brownie's kind of clumsy for that sort of a job."

Hig scratched his head. "I doubt there's much danger of anyone callin' him quick on his feet or quick-witted either one."

"No, but he can still be trouble."

"He won't with me." Hig smoked his cigarette right down to his fingertips. He blew out the smoke and said, "You go about whatever you need to do. When me an' Gene get back with the horses, we'll get started on the chuck wagon." He arched an eyebrow. "We don't have much more time."

Dunbar set down his coffee cup. "I know," he said.

I looked across at Rumsey, and he gave me an expression that said he didn't know a thing. That made two of us. I didn't know what Dunbar had in mind for us to do, and I didn't know why Hig was sending me along.

Dunbar and I went out into the brisk morning. He brushed and saddled the blue roan while I got the deep-chested sorrel ready. No one said anything about staying out overnight, so when I had my horse saddled I led him into the yard and waited to mount up. Dunbar came out of the barn in his untroubled way, with his head up, his arms and shoulders relaxed, and his reins loose in his gloved right hand.

"Go get a shovel and tie it on the back of your saddle," he said.

I frowned. "Have you got some digging in mind?"

"That's the main use of a shovel." He reached out his left

hand, also gloved, and held my reins for me as I went on my errand.

Having a shovel on top of my slicker across the back of my saddle was a nuisance, as I had to distort the way I swung my leg up and over. I had seen fellows who, when they had a bundle or another person on the back of the saddle, could draw the right leg between the left leg and the saddle, swing the right boot over the saddle horn, and get mounted that way. But I did not have any such tricks, so I had to swing my leg back, up, and around. The deep-chested sorrel was a placid horse, though, so he was still in the same spot when I came down into my seat.

To my surprise, we set off toward the northwest. I thought we would find very few Little Six cattle where the Rim angled away in that direction, but I figured Dunbar had a plan. Also, I gathered that he didn't want to answer a lot of questions.

I rode on, with the sorrel keeping pace about half a length back from the blue roan. The morning stayed cool for quite a while, with a high cloud cover. A medium-strength breeze, not strong and not light, blew out of the northwest and carried a hint of moisture. I had my denim jacket buttoned all the way up, and I kept my hatbrim tilted against the wind, even when I scanned the country around us.

After an hour and a half of riding, we stopped at a windmill and dismounted. I knew it belonged to a man named Owens and we were crossing his land, but no one begrudged his neighbor a drink of water in this country. Dunbar had gotten to know several people and a great many things in the short while he had been here, and I imagined he knew who owned the windmill, but again I didn't make any comments or ask questions.

The water tank was three feet wide and eight feet long, like a large coffin or catafalque. It was made of posts and planks, lined inside with sheet metal, and caulked with gobs of tar. The water was clear, and although the wind ruffled the surface, I could see all the way down. As with many such tanks, the white skulls and bones of birds lay undisturbed on the bottom. Overhead, the blades creaked in the wind, making a lonely sound in this spot on the prairie. The rod groaned and thumped as it moved up and down, and at the far end of the tank from where we watered our horses, a trickle of water splashed in from a stub of pipe.

Although the day had not yet warmed up, Dunbar took off his dark, high-crowned hat and set it on his saddle horn. With his gloves in his coat pocket, he bent toward the tank and splashed water on his face. He rubbed the water from his eyes, blinked, and smoothed his bushy mustache. He shook his hands and squared his shoulders, took a deep breath and gave a look around at the countryside.

As he waved his hands to dry them off, I saw again the dark spot in his palm. As usual, he did not seem to be either hiding it or showing it; rather, he seemed not to be conscious of it. I let my own thoughts drift as I, too, gazed at the dull landscape.

His voice brought me back. "So, what's eatin' you, kid?"

I wanted to say that I didn't like him going off on his own and, to all appearances, spending time with Ruth. But I didn't dare, so I said, "Nothing."

"There's somethin'," he said, not quite as offhand but still casual. "You might as well get it out."

"I doubt that Hig sent me along for that. For whatever reason he did, I'm not sure."

"Well, you *are* peeved. That's evident." He put on his hat, tugged the brim, and turned his dark eyes on me. "Hig sent you along because you and I work together. It's as simple as that. But if I work with a man, I want to know if he's got something against me."

I didn't doubt him on that, but I was sure he didn't have to go through question and answer with every man he worked with. "I don't have anything against you," I said.

"There's something. I've got to be able to trust you, so spit it out."

I was sure he was still just working me, but I felt I had to say something. So I cleared my throat and said, "It's probably none of my business, but I get tired of things being so mysterious."

His dark eyes bore down on me. "Like what?"

"Like your coming and going and being who knows where."

"I've got things to do on my own, you know."

I shrugged. "So it seems."

He had his gloves on now, and he stood with his hands on his hips, the reins dangling from his left hand. "Well, that's hardly enough. Let's hear the rest of it."

I felt he was needling me, so with a bit of pique I said, "If you hadn't been off on your own, Tim Odell might not have gotten killed."

Dunbar let out a heavy breath. "Oh, that. Well, I'm sorry for what happened to him, but I didn't cause it. I might have been able to head it off if I had been there, but a man can't be everywhere at all times. And like I told Hig, Falke's carryin' out orders. I'm sure he picked out Odell from that earlier run-in we had. He saw that Tim was a quick one to rile, and I'd guess he waited until I wasn't around and then he took his chance. Sure, Falke goaded him into it, but Odell went for his gun first, so there's not much anyone can do about it now."

I pushed my own argument, even as I knew it was not my real complaint. "I think they were looking for you and took it out on him."

Dunbar, still unruffled, said, "Too bad they didn't find me. If they're that good, they should have known how."

"Huh," I said, as I drew the slack in my reins and went to turn my horse around. I stopped as his voice came back at me.

"Look here, Grey. I can tell you've got somethin' else eatin' on you, and I might even have a hunch what it is, but it doesn't have to come between you and me and the work we've got to do."

I gave him a look that said I didn't agree, and I believe he read it straight.

"So go ahead and feed it for a while. But when you come around, I think you'll see that what you want and what I want are pretty close together." He was not being stern with me, and as he gave me a nod of the head, his eyebrows raised and he made a half-smile.

It's hard to argue when a fellow has to do it all himself. We led our horses out a few steps and mounted up. As I swung my leg back and then up and over, I wondered again what the shovel was for. But I figured I would find out soon enough.

Our ride took us out to where the bluffs broke up into hard-scrabble breaks. The grass was sparse, and I saw no fresh sign of cattle or horses. We took noon rest at the foot of a rocky draw, where I was pretty sure there was not a tree within miles. The cloud cover was thinning overhead, and the sun seemed to be struggling to break through. The horses stood on their own faint shadows as Dunbar and I sat with our backs to the breeze and ate cold biscuits.

Out of the blue, he asked a question in his casual tone. "What do you think of what Hig said about Brownie?"

I was surprised he asked for my opinion. "I don't know," I said. "I would guess he got it from Lon Buckley, so it's probably more dependable than if he got it from—I don't know, Redington."

"Do you think there's anything to dig up?"

Again he took me off guard. "About Whipple?" I asked.

"Yeh."

I shook my head. "I don't know. He goes from one place to the next. I guess he could leave a bad taste—or I should say, bad feelings. You've talked to Ruth. You know what I mean. It seems as if there's always something she thinks she has to apologize for. So he might have left someone holding the bag at some point or another."

"Do you think he's a crook?"

I hesitated. "That would be a strong thing for me to say to one man about another."

"But you know he does crooked things. From what we've found together, and what you've seen on your own."

"Well," I said, "if you know it, that should be good enough."

Dunbar smiled. "You'll do all right, Grey."

"Then what's the shovel for?"

He laughed. "Why, to dig things up."

After our noon rest, we mounted our horses and backtracked, drifting through the rough, broken country until we came again to the bluffs where the formation of Decker Rim began. Dunbar studied the ground just as he had when we rode over it earlier. He meandered here and there, with me sometimes following and sometimes waiting. When we moved onto new ground, at least new for us on that day, he traveled even slower than before. I was careful not to get ahead of him, as I didn't want to track up the ground. From time to time he would step down from the saddle, crouch, and study closer. He pulled at the grass, poked at the dirt, rolled rocks one way and another.

We ambled along the rough wall. When it cut inward to a cleft or side canyon, we followed. The sky overhead had cleared, and I could feel the warmth reflected off of the wall as the sun still hung at its high point. Cottontail rabbits darted from one shady spot to another. In one inlet that looked like a box canyon, a black-tail doe and her fawn jumped up, bounding in the tall brush, and disappeared in a crack in the wall.

Shadows began to creep out from the base of the bluffs. The afternoon grew warm and stayed quiet, with no sounds except the footfalls of our horses and the occasional wheeze of a hawk overhead. The slowness of it all made me drowsy. I saw grass and cactus, rocks and bushes; I saw walls rise up, with tufts of grass and clumps of rabbit brush growing on tiny ledges. On the floor of one side canyon, the dead pods of a yucca plant rose out of a cluster of bayonets. Sagebrush hung heavy, and trails of small critters made their sandy way through the grass and other lower growth. I was seeing all of this through dull, heavy-lidded eyes when Dunbar's voice traveled on the air.

"Over here."

My eyes opened, and I reined my horse in Dunbar's direction. He swung down from the roan and held it aside as he peered at the ground. I rode to within five yards of him and dismounted.

"Looks like someone's done some diggin' here," he said.

I nodded. I wouldn't have minded splashing some water on my face at that moment, but we were in a hot, dry canyon where the air didn't move, so I just took in a deep breath of air to see if I could clear my head. I gazed at the area of disturbed dirt and wondered if it was big enough to hold a body.

"Get the shovel," said Dunbar, reaching a gloved hand to take my reins.

I took down the shovel and went to work as he told me. It was a short tool with a "D" handle, so I had to bend over with every stab and scrape. The dirt was loose, but it had wads of grass and chunks of hard earth mixed in, so the shovel head sometimes skidded and sometimes came to an abrupt stop. I dug on as Dunbar stood holding the reins of the two horses. My face sweated, and dust rose in the air around me. I moved to the other side of the hole, wiped my face, and kept digging.

About a foot down, the blade of the shovel started hitting

something irregular. The object had some give to it, but it was at least a couple of feet long and was embedded in the dirt. From the way it moved and shifted, I did not think it was a sack of stagecoach money. I had an uncertain feeling, as I thought I might be pushing against the arm and leg of a human being or a lump of hide and guts from a range cow.

I dug and scraped, and a patch of dark hair came into view. Short hair, with dirt falling out of it as I poked the lump with my shovel. I dug to the right, then to the left. I could tell it was a hide, and I felt less squeamish as I scraped away dirt and pried at the edges of the heap.

"Go ahead and pull it out," said Dunbar.

I strained and sweated, as folds of the hide were weighed down with the offal. Guts and feet tumbled back into the hole, with dirt spilling in as well, as I dragged out the hide and attached head of a brownish-black animal. As I pulled it free, I saw the Little Six brand on its left hip.

"Looks like a yearling. Roll that hide over. Yep, it's a heifer."

"Not the one you heard about before."

"No, it was a brindle, or so they said. And this one's not been here but a few days. The blood's still red."

"What shall we do with it?"

Dunbar tipped his hat back. "We ought to be able to just leave it here, and even if someone came along and found it and then got rid of it, your word and mine ought to be good enough. All the same, I think we'll stash it. Go ahead and fill in that hole, and make sure you cover up everything—except the hide, of course. Leave it right there for the moment."

I had not yet caught my breath, and there I was, moving dirt again, making clouds of dust that rose into my sweaty face.

All this time, Dunbar stood back holding the horses and keeping clean. He did not have a great air of satisfaction about him. Rather, he seemed to be exercising his patience until he could get on to the next step.

When I had the dirt back in place and tromped down, I took the shovel to the back of my horse and tied it on. Coming around front by Dunbar, I stopped to take a breather. I set my hat cocked and tilted for ventilation and dragged my sleeve across my forehead. Then I took down my canteen and had a drink of water.

As I screwed the cap back on, Dunbar spoke.

"Put your rope around the neck of that thing, and we'll drag it up top and find a place to leave it."

I felt myself getting perturbed again. I could understand him bringing me along for a witness and to do some of the digging, but I didn't appreciate him letting me do all the dirty work. I remembered telling Tut Whipple that Dunbar didn't dig ditches, and now I wondered how much I should admire his repose. Maybe Dunbar did, as Ruth suggested, want to show others he was superior. Then it occurred to me that perhaps for some subtle reason he didn't want to touch the evidence himself. It was hard to guess what he wanted. As I slipped the rope around the neck of the animal where the head was attached to the rest of the hide, I thought of Dunbar's earlier comment that what he and I wanted were close to the same. I didn't think this was quite it.

He had mounted up by the time I rose with the slack of my rope in my hands. He held out my reins, and I took them. With my right arm around the neck of my horse I got the reins and rope in place, then pulled myself aboard. I dallied up and followed Dunbar to the far end of the little canyon. There we climbed a slope and came out on the flats above.

The air was lighter than down below, and the breeze felt good on my face. We rode across curling grass to the next place where the wall cut inward. There Dunbar found a crevice that met with his approval.

"Roll it up in a bundle and stuff it in there," he said as he pointed.

I was glad I was wearing gloves, as the hide was moist on the underside, where the blood was red, the fat was slick, and dirt had stuck to the wet spots. The hide had a hint of a rotten smell to it as well, and it shifted in my hands when I had it rolled up and hoisted to knee level. I walked bent over, and when I came to the washout I settled the bundle down into it on a ledge.

"That should be good for a while," said Dunbar. "If we need it."

He led the way back down the trail we had come up, and in a few minutes we were riding along the base of the bluffs again. The shadows reached out a couple of feet by now, and I figured we were less than a mile from the place where Whipple's crew was moving dirt. I wondered why we didn't cut across country and head for the ranch, but Dunbar, who seemed to know every nook and cranny out there, kept us riding along the wall. Now and again he would draw up behind a formation that jutted out, and from there he would watch the landscape before riding out into the open.

During one of those pauses, as I sat vacant-minded on my horse, Dunbar motioned with his hand. I thought he meant for me to come forward, but as I nudged my horse, he held out his hand to stop me. Then I saw what he was indicating to me.

Two riders were crossing the rangeland at a fast walk. The taller one rode a sand-colored horse, and his tan, high-crowned hat bobbed in the afternoon sunlight. The other man, dressed in brown, sat slouched in the saddle, a dumpy figure in a bowler hat. I imagined Falke was escorting Brownie back to town.

Dunbar and I stayed put until the other two had ridden out of sight. Then Dunbar took us out into the open. Within ten minutes we came to the main trail, where Dunbar turned right and led the way up on top again.

Paused in the cooling breeze, we looked down at the work project. The crew had been making progress, all right. The teams had scraped and scoured the entire floor of the reservoir and were now cutting deeper. Off to the southwest, a two-horse team and a four-horse team were lengthening the scar of the canal.

I could pick out Tut Whipple below. He kept his back to us, but I was sure he knew we were there. Stiver, who was at his side, looked at us two or three times and kept talking to the boss. But Whipple did not turn. Even at that distance, I knew his method. If he didn't recognize us, we weren't there.

Dunbar led the way back down the trail, and when we were a mile away from the work site, we set off across country toward the ranch.

When we got there, three of the vagrant horses stood in the corral, and Rumsey had the fourth one snubbed close to a heavy post. It was a grayish-white horse with a charcoal-colored mane and tail. Rumsey stood at the animal's hip and pulled a steel comb through the long strands of the tail. He smiled and waved as we took our horses to the barn for unsaddling.

At supper, as we worked our way through tough beef and fried potatoes, Hig was thoughtful. He would chew and stop and ask a question, then chew and stop and say a word or two. When he had gotten the full report from Dunbar, he said, "They don't quit, do they?"

"Doesn't seem like it," said Dunbar. "They had a warning, and they went right along and did it again. At least once."

Hig's narrow eyes were fixed on the coffee pot. "I suppose someone needs to go into town tomorrow, then."

"I can do it," said Dunbar.

"Best not go alone."

"Oh, I can take Grey. He's handy to have along. Does all the work."

Hig poked his finger inside his crusted bandanna and rubbed his neck. "Well, don't take all day if you don't have to. Gene's got these horses to work with, and we need to get the wagon ready."

"We won't waste time," said Dunbar.

I believed him. I could feel in the air that things were moving toward some point, even though I didn't know what it was.

CHAPTER ELEVEN

Riding the brown ranch horse, I followed Dunbar on his buckskin as we entered town on the east side of the pond. The wall of dirt rose on my left, and shoots of green grass appeared on the pocked surface. A thin stream of water poured out of the headgate and flowed down the spillway, and as I rode over the stone bridge and saw the course of rocks I had planted at the base of the dam, I tried to imagine how much water was being held in place. The whole structure impressed me with its stability and permanence, something that was here to stay and could be depended on.

At the top of the hill, Dunbar paused to look across the surface of the pond, and I did the same. The sun on my back gave me a hint of warmth. Then I saw Dunbar's face tighten, as if something had come to the surface of his memory, and he turned the buckskin and spurred it toward town.

We turned at the corner with the livery stable on our left, and Dunbar headed for the hitching rail in front of the Whitepaw Saloon. The mid-morning sun had begun to warm the air in the main street, and the businesses along each side showed signs of life. A barrel of brooms and mops sat on the sidewalk in front of Fenn Fuller's mercantile, and his clerk came to the doorway, all the better to report to his boss who these men were who were going into the saloon at this time of day. Three doors down, Al Redington came to the door of his butcher shop and got a look for himself.

Straight across from the meat market, on the right side of the saloon, the druggist had hung out a wicker cage with a large, blue-green parrot that looked as unkempt as a buzzard. As we stepped up onto the sidewalk, the bird creaked out three syllables that sounded like "pretty boy." Dunbar gave it a sideways glance and made a short, liquid, whistling sound. Then our bootheels thumped as we walked toward the saloon.

The front door was propped open with a wooden bucket of mop water, so we went in without ceremony. Although the place was airing out, it had the stale smell of a saloon in the morning, and the light that came in through the doorway gave the interior a pasty tone.

Lon Buckley stood in back of the bar, where he was pulling out partially full bottles and setting them on the bar top. His swamper, a toothless old man who walked hunched over, was carrying a kerosene lamp from the bar to a table. Above the bar, in the pale light filtering upward, the bobcat looked like just another stuffed animal, while the Indian with the uplifted knife made me feel as if I had walked in on some tawdry act.

Lon's face carried an indefinite expression as he asked, "Somethin' I can do for you?"

"Have you got coffee?" asked Dunbar.

"I can make some."

"That would be good."

Lon called to his swamper. "Mason! Build up a fire and get a pot of coffee goin'." Then he brought his eyes back to us and said, "Anything with it?"

"I don't think so," said Dunbar. He turned to me. "Do you want a shot of whiskey with yours?"

"I'll pass," I said.

Dunbar and I moved to a table next to the one where the council usually sat. Lon went back to taking stock of his liquor. Now and then I heard the bump of a bottle being set on the bar top or the clink of one bottle touching another, but otherwise the place had a vacant feeling to it. We sat at the table for about ten minutes until Mason came out from the back room and began moving and adjusting chairs with very little purpose. When he came near us, Dunbar spoke.

"Do you think you could take a message for me?"

The old man turned his bleary eyes on Dunbar. His mouth flapped as he said, "If it's anywhere here in town."

"Sure," said Dunbar. He gave an easy smile. "It's just across the street." He took a two-bit piece from his pocket and handed it to the man. "My name's Dunbar," he went on, "and I'd like you to tell Mr. Fuller and Mr. Redington that I've got somethin' that could blow this town wide open, and I think they'd like to talk to me first."

The old man raised his thin eyebrows and said, "I'll tell 'em."

Lon Buckley stood motionless with a bottle of whiskey in both hands like a statuette he was about to show. His light-colored eyes went from the swamper to Dunbar, and then he moved to put the bottle on a shelf behind the bar.

Mason came back within a few minutes. "They'll be here," he said, giving a firm gesture with his toothless mouth.

Dunbar nodded.

"Go see to the coffee," said Buckley. "Bring some cups. Five or six."

Mason was setting the crockery mugs on the bar when Fenn Fuller came in through the bright doorway. He was dressed in a lightweight tan suit and his dark brown derby.

"Have a seat," said Dunbar.

I could tell that Fenn didn't like to be told to sit somewhere other than his accustomed place, but he took a seat with his back to the west wall. As he took off his hat, he looked at me and said, "Good morning, Grey."

"Good morning."

"I hope you're not getting into things you'll wish you hadn't." His eyes bore down on me through the gold-rimmed spectacles.

"The kid's just doin' his work," said Dunbar. "Hig sent him along, and he's a great help. But if there's anything to be regretted, I'll answer for it."

"We'll see."

A large shape blocked out some of the sunlight as Redington came through the doorway. He glanced at Fuller, then at Buckley, and took a seat opposite me. "So what's the uproar?" he asked.

Lon was setting empty cups in front of us, bending forward each time as he moved around the table. When he was out of Dunbar's line of vision, Dunbar said, "I discovered something that I think someone needs to be called to account for."

Redington, who had a heavy, tired look to his face and was breathing with his mouth open, said, "I hope it's more substantial than the last time."

"I believe it is," said Dunbar.

Fenn Fuller's eyebrows went up as he widened his eyes. "I heard about your last complaint. A bit circumstantial at best, mostly hearsay." He stretched his chin forward and lifted it as he gave a condescending look. "Rather empty declarations."

"Maybe I'll put it in the form of a question, then."

Fenn took out his watch, pursed his lips, and said, "Oh, go ahead." Then he opened his watch and looked at it.

"Why don't you bring in a lawman? Hire a town marshal."

Fuller's eyes came up. "What for?"

"To look into obvious wrong-doings."

The bluish-gray eyes went hard behind the spectacles, and Fuller's mouth moved forward. "What wrong might that be?"

Dunbar looked square at him and said, "The appropriation of someone's range animals and the illegal conveyance of slaughtered beef."

Redington shifted in his seat.

Fuller said, "You speak like a lawyer."

"Well, I'm not one."

"Maybe you should study it some. Learn that you need evidence to back up your accusations." Fuller closed his watch with a click and put it away. He raised his cup, took a sip, and said, "Well?"

Dunbar turned his dark eyes on Redington and then Fuller. "Both of you know well enough that we've had problems. Higgins has cause to believe that the ditch crew has been making free with his cattle, and there's also reason to believe that they've had some help workin' up a bill of sale now and then."

Fuller adjusted his spectacles. "Be careful of what you say."

"The truth comes easy, and here it is." Dunbar took a drink of coffee and went on. "Yesterday, while Grey and I were out riding, we found where someone had buried the hide and guts of a yearling heifer. Had the Little Six brand on it."

Fuller gave a tiny shrug.

"It's not the one I raised the question about before. The other one was a brindle, or so I'd been told. This one was dark, and the kill was just a day or two old." After a pause, Dunbar added, "If you want evidence, we've got it."

"I don't think you understand," said Fuller. "I don't doubt that someone helped himself to one of your boss's animals, but it's hard to prove who did it or where the beef went. That's where you need the reasonable evidence."

"So, even if I have evidence that the crime was committed, no one wants to look into it. That's it, isn't it?"

Fuller turned in his seat, and his thinning hair and reddish-gray side-whiskers caught the light that straggled from the door. "I don't have any jurisdiction here," he said. "And even if I did, it wouldn't reach out to the rangeland where this thing was done."

Dunbar's face showed irritation as he said, "There are things that go on, right here under your nose, and you don't want to know about them."

I looked from Fuller's button nose to Redington's bulbous growth, purple at the sides of the nostrils. I could tell the butcher was uneasy.

Fuller gave a frown. "Don't get me wrong. If there's a problem in this town, and I mean *in* this town, I want to know about it. But I want proof that it happened. Now, you say we should bring in a lawman. Some towns do that, when they've got problems. Same thing on the range. Cattlemen bring in a stock detective. So there's a leaf from your own book. And if your boss wants to bring in the law, he's free to ask the sheriff to send out a deputy from Cheyenne." Fuller looked satisfied with himself, as if he had won the argument in everyone's eyes.

I let my glance travel from Fuller to Redington to Buckley. It was clear to me that they had things worked out so that an answer would be ready whenever it was needed. None of this conversation seemed to take Lon Buckley by surprise, which led me to think that the saloon-keeper didn't tell his old friend Higgins everything.

"You know how likely that is," said Dunbar. "Send a deputy on a two-day ride to investigate a butchered animal."

Fuller shrugged. "You have that option."

"You know it's not realistic. And as for the rest of the problem, you don't seem to want to know about it."

"I think I've made our position clear," said Fuller. "If I may presume to speak on behalf of others than myself."

"Well, you've heard ours, too, and I think you can assume you haven't heard the last. About this, or other matters."

"Oh, really?" A flush rose on Fuller's cheeks. "Something that pertains to us, I hope."

"It all does. Whether you want to see it or not."

That stopped Fuller, but for only a second. He recovered and said, "Well, if that's all for the time being, we can get back to our work." He gave his bowler hat a half-twirl and put it on his head. "So much for the urgency. I hope there's more to it next time."

A shape at the doorway cut off some of the light, and everyone turned to see Brownie making his entrance. It seemed as if he was trying to be jaunty, although his weight pulled him forward and he walked in his flat-footed way.

"What's the ruckus?" he asked.

"Nothing," said Fuller. "Al and I were just going."

"Was this fella givin' you any trouble?" Brownie's voice, loud and flat, was abrasive as always.

"Not trouble," came the firm answer as Fenn lifted his chin. Then looking around the table, he said, "Gentlemen, good day."

As he and Redington made their way outside, Lon Buckley moved his eyes toward Brownie. The man came forward, wagging his head as he cast a glance over our table.

"Anything I can serve you?" asked Buckley.

"Nah, I just came in to see if this one was causin' trouble."

Lon Buckley was a picture of calm. His slender build stood in neat contrast with Brownie's, and he was dressed as usual in his white shirt, arm garters, gray vest, and matching pants. His gray hair was combed up and back, and his sallow-toned face showed no expression. "Like Fenn said, we don't have trouble in here."

Brownie had come close and now stood at Dunbar's elbow. I could feel the man's bulky presence even from where I sat. He tipped his head to one side and gave Dunbar an insolent look. "I heard him say that."

"Maybe he meant it," said Dunbar.

"Yeah, yeah. Everyone does."

Dunbar did not move in his chair as he gave a dark glare

upward and said, "Don't crowd me."

Brownie shifted on his feet as if he was going to move closer.

Dunbar rose in a split second and stood inches from the other man's face. "I said, don't crowd me."

"I could put a hole right through you," said Brownie.

"You need a lot more practice with that cheap pistol. Don't try it with me."

Brownie must have seen something in Dunbar's eyes that I couldn't from where I was sitting. The sneer vanished from Brownie's face. He looked up and down, turned, and walked away.

I stole a glance at Lon Buckley, who was keeping a close eye on Dunbar. The saloon-keeper had no doubt seen a few hard men, even in a town like Winsome, and I could sense that he did not despise Dunbar. He just wanted to see what the man would do.

We left town the way we came in, past the pond and over the stone bridge. The sun had climbed a little more, and I could feel the warmth of it on the side of my horse's neck, but I still took a while to get over the chill of sitting in the cold, gloomy saloon. From time to time I hunched my shoulders and tensed my upper body, and my jacket held in the warmth I generated. By the time everything seemed to be flowing again, we were going through the hills that lay south of town.

Dunbar was riding easy, the reins loose in his gloved hand. His canvas coat was open, but his vest was buttoned snug. I imagined he was planning his next move, and I wondered how far he was going to pursue this case. It seemed serious enough when we dug up the hide, but when it came to trying to get something done about it, I could see that it didn't matter much to the outer world. I knew Hig wanted to get results before we went on roundup, but I had my doubts.

I lapsed into other thoughts as I pictured the horses I would be riding for the next six weeks. My stomach tightened as I recalled the last one in my string, a hammer-headed white horse that I never trusted. More than once he tried to run out from under me, and I knew he could feel my tenseness every time I climbed on.

I took a deep breath and reached forward to pat the neck of the brown horse I was riding. As I leaned, something in the air snapped.

My horse jerked to the left, almost spilling me, as the crash of a rifle shot followed the splitting of the air. The horse plunged in front, kicked up in back, and pulled away from Dunbar and the buckskin. I grabbed the saddle horn and let my horse run. Dunbar's, meanwhile, had reared up and come down bucking. I didn't look back because it took all I had to hold on. I had lost my left stirrup and was bouncing from one side of the saddle to the other. Another shot sounded, but it was way in back of me.

The brown horse slowed from a dead run to a gallop, and I was working to get my boot back in the stirrup when I heard Dunbar coming up behind me. Then he was alongside, keeping pace.

"Are you all right?" he hollered.

"Yeah, I'm fine. And you?" I couldn't see any blood on him or his horse, but I couldn't take more than a glance at a time.

"Oh, I'm all right, but I sure don't like it." He had his head bent into the wind, and I could see a grave look on his face.

We covered a mile in a short time, with no more shots after the first two. Dunbar slowed his horse to a walk, and I did likewise.

"Who do you think it was?" I asked.

"Don't know. But I don't think it was anyone we talked to earlier."

"Not Brownie?"

"It could be, but I don't think so. I don't think he had time to go get a horse, wait for it to be saddled, and then go for a rifle, all in plain view."

"How would someone else have gotten wind of it that quick?"

Dunbar shook his head. "I don't know. Someone like the honest butcher might have been able to pass on the word as we sat in there drinkin' our coffee."

"But that means someone would have had to have been nearby and ready to go."

He shrugged. "They could have been waitin' anyway."

"Before they even knew you were going to spring this thing?"

Dunbar shook his head again. "Hard to tell at this point." He reined his horse to a stop. "But I'd bet they're gone now. We can go take a look."

I turned my horse around and followed him, still at a walk. He pointed to the southeast.

"Whoever it was, he or they, was probably shootin' from that point there. It's closest to the trail."

Dunbar led the way to the back side of the row of hills, and we took it slow and careful as we came up behind the vantage point he had indicated. The hillside had good grass, so there weren't many hoofprints to be seen, but the dirt was bare in a couple of places. Dunbar got down to go on foot, and I did the same.

"Looks like just one horse," he said. "Unshod."

"It wouldn't be from the livery stable, then. He runs shoes on all the ones he has for hire. And like you said before, it's hard to imagine Brownie coming out here on a fast ride, even if it was on some other horse."

We walked up the hill and looked out over the narrow valley. The trail lay in clear view, down and about three hundred yards away.

Dunbar nodded, then pointed with his gloved hand. "Looks

like he laid on the grass right here. Don't see any casings, though. Must have picked 'em up. Be stupid not to."

I felt a chill across my shoulders as I gazed at the trail where we had ridden by just a little while earlier. "Likely place," I said.

"Yeh, and when it came right down to it, he couldn't draw a fine enough bead. But he tried."

We walked down the back of the hill, and when we got to level ground, Dunbar turned around and studied the layout.

"See something?" I asked.

"No, but it's always good to take a second look. Some people, you know, they study maps upside-down. Others I've heard of will bend over and look at the landscape behind 'em, through their legs. I've tried that one, but it doesn't work well for me. But a second glance is worth it. It's like studyin' the land in back of you when you ride through new country, see what it looks like if you're comin' the other way."

I nodded.

"You know someone was here," he said, "but the land is like a deaf mute. It sees and knows, but it won't give up a thing." His face was dead serious as his eyes met mine. "I don't like bein' shot at," he said. "Even a clod-hopper can hit his mark once in a while, and no one fires a shot like this without havin' a clear intention."

I raised my head and looked around, gazing far beyond Decker Rim to the west, where the Laramie Mountains rose against a blue sky. In all this wide land, one man had come sneaking out to take shots at another. It seemed to me that the problem of a few head of rustled beef had gotten out of proportion.

"So what do we do, then?" I asked.

Dunbar pushed his lips together, and his bushy mustache went up. "We go back to town."

Chapter Twelve

We rode back through the hills toward town, and when we came out into the open, the settlement lay ahead of us as always—a cluster of buildings on a grassy plain, where people came together to make a living and get through life. The roofs reflected the sunlight, and from a few stovepipes, the wisps of smoke rose on the air and dissipated. Downslope from the town and closer to the hills we rode out of, the pond sparkled with the bright blue color of the sky.

When Dunbar and the buckskin came to a stop, I drew rein alongside. Dunbar seemed to be contemplating the scene, or rather its contents. After a long moment he nudged the horse into motion again. We went down the slope at a fast walk until we came to the place where the trail forked to go around either side of the pond.

Dunbar motioned with his head toward the left. "I'll go this way," he said. "I'll meet you in about an hour, in front of the Whitepaw. I imagine you can find somethin' to do."

My head went back an inch as if I had caught a gust of wind. He was going around the west end, over the plank bridge and up the slope toward Ruth's place, and he was sending me off on my own. After a couple of seconds, the words came to me. "I suppose so."

"All right. We'll see you." He made a clicking sound, and the buckskin took off at a lope.

I went on around the east end, and for some reason I didn't

feel like crossing the stone bridge. I meandered down the ditch a ways until I found a spot where other animals had crossed. As I turned the brown horse down the ditchbank, he decided he didn't want to cross the water. He bunched up and would not go forward. He turned his head and front feet from one side to another as I spurred him, and then in a suspended moment he gathered up, lurched, and cleared the little stream. We landed with a whoof and a rustling of leather, and he scrambled up the other side. Now he was fine, and he picked up his feet as we headed toward the entrance to town.

We took the slope at an angle, and as we came to the street, the glittering pile of empty bottles in back of the saloon came into view. I turned and rode to the main street, and when I came to the corner with the blacksmith shop on my right, I turned again. Twenty yards away, out in plain view, a crow sat on the arch of the fire bell. He watched me as I turned.

Across the street, Henry Dornick's crew was working on the west side of the bank building. A stout wooden scaffold stood against the outside wall, and two men were lifting a rectangular chunk of quarried stone. They lifted the piece above their heads, where two men on the scaffold reached down for it. In the background I could hear what sounded like a hand sledge hitting the head of a chisel.

I rode on toward the Castle as the plink-plink of the hammer and chisel was joined by a half-dozen ringing blows from the blacksmith shop. Then the sounds faded behind me, and I heard the cawing of the crow as he flapped overhead. After that the town was quiet. I wondered if a train line would ever lay tracks this way, and I grimaced as I thought of the noise it would bring. Much better this way, I thought, when a fellow could hear a crow, or meadowlarks a stone's throw out on the prairie, or the whirling cries of the sandhill cranes when they came in early fall.

My horse's hooves tick-tocked on the dry, packed dirt, and I realized a tune was running through my mind. It was the one I had heard on an earlier visit to the Castle.

Meet me tonight in the moonlight,
Leave your little sister at home.
Meet me out back of the churchyard,
Don't leave me to wait all alone.

It was the only stanza I could remember, and it played through several times.

The sun warmed my back as I swayed in the saddle. I was still wearing my jacket, and I hoped the inside of the Castle was more pleasant than the Whitepaw Saloon had been a couple of hours earlier. My horse's shadow told me we were past noon, which meant that the cookstove would have been going for a while. That, and the prospect of a few minutes' conversation, should get me through the hour pretty well.

Two men came out of the roadhouse, untied their horses, and rode away to the east. The hitching rail was now vacant. I dismounted and tied my horse, then went into the Castle. Clark, the proprietor, was seated at a table with a ledger open in front of him. He put his finger on the page as he looked up and around.

"Come to eat?"

"If I'm not too late."

"Oh, no."

I made my way to the table by the window, where I usually sat when I came by myself. Clark called out to Rachel, and within a minute she appeared from the dim area in back.

Her hair hung loose at her shoulders, not quite covering the earrings of dark blue stone. She wore a dress that matched the earrings, and although she wore a dull white apron over it, I appreciated her figure well enough.

"Good afternoon," she said. Then, with her eyes sparkling, she asked, "Are you a hungry boy today?"

"I don't know. That is, I haven't thought much about it. It's that time of day, and I had an hour on my hands, so it seemed like the thing to do. What's good today?"

She smiled. "Meat and gravy. Mashed potatoes. Biscuits."

"Can't argue with that." Then I remembered some greasy pork gravy I had had one time in the café downtown. "What kind of meat?" I asked.

"Beef. It came from the butcher shop this morning."

I met her eyes and smiled. "Should be fine."

I watched her walk away, and then I gazed out the window. A yellowish milk cow walked across the empty lot, followed by a bony white cow with a dry bag. The grass in the lot had been cropped pretty close, and the cows were on their way, none too fast, to better grazing.

From across the room where he sat with his ledger, Clark made a coughing sound from the bottom of his throat. A voice rose in the kitchen, followed by the whacking of a spoon on the lip of a pot. When I looked out the window again, the cows had disappeared.

Rachel came from the kitchen with a plate of meat and gravy in one hand and a smaller plate of biscuits in the other. As she came closer, I could see that the gravy covered a cratered mound of potatoes.

"Looks good," I said as she set the food in front of me.

She straightened up and said, "It should be." A clanging sound came from the kitchen. "Anything else?" she asked.

"Not at the moment."

"I'll be back later, then." She turned and went to the kitchen.

I dug into my meal, and it roused my appetite. The meat was a bit tough, which was to be expected if it was cut up to be cooked in gravy, but it had been seared well and had a good pan-fried flavor. The gravy had cooked a while, too, so it was not the kind of pale sop that some places served.

Clark made his coughing sound again, took out his watch and opened it, and snapped it shut. He pushed himself up from the table and cleared his throat, then stood for a moment as he took off his glasses and put them in his vest pocket. He went to the end of the bar, where he picked up a newspaper, and from there he went out the back door.

I had cleaned my plate and had two biscuits left when Rachel emerged from the kitchen. She was carrying a crockery jam pot that had a notch in the lid and the handle of a small wooden spoon sticking out.

"I almost forgot this," she said.

"I'm glad you didn't." I glanced at the empty table where her boss had been sitting. "You're not in a hurry, are you?"

She pushed out her lower lip and gave a slow shake of the head. "Oh, no."

"Would you like to sit down?" I nodded at the chair across from me.

"No, I'll stand. But go ahead."

After separating one of the biscuits with my fork, I took the lid off the crockery dish. The jam was reddish purple with bits of fruit skin in the texture, and I guessed it was plum. I dipped out a spoonful.

"I don't get to talk to you very much," I said. "I've enjoyed the parties, though. Good food, and everybody treats me well."

The corners of her eyes crinkled, and she made a faint smile. "You know how it is. My mother is very protective."

"Oh, sure. That's normal."

"More than she used to be."

"Oh?"

"Ever since what happened to Annie Mora."

A shiver went through me, and I paused with the wooden

spoon between my finger and thumb. I raised my eyes to meet Rachel's. "I'm very sorry about that. About her, I mean, and the way people have shrugged it off." After a pause I added, "They say she probably ran off."

"I know." Rachel's eyes were dark and serious. "Do you think she did?"

I shrugged. "Not really. Do you?"

"No, and her family doesn't think so, either. And my father, he asks everywhere he goes, and no one has seen her."

"I truly am sorry," I said, "but I don't know what I can do. If I did, I would." I met her eyes again. "I hope your mother doesn't think I'm the type who would do something."

She smiled. "Well, you're a boy, and all boys can do something."

"I guess."

"And she says that cow-boys are as bad as any. No responsibility. One day they're here, and the next day they're gone far away."

"Well, I suppose some of them are like that. But I'm not, and I don't expect to be. As far as that goes, I don't expect to be a cowpuncher all my life, either."

"Oh?"

I shrugged, lighter this time. "It's work for a while, but I expect to go on to something else."

"What do you plan to do?"

"It's not definite," I said. "You know, you try on one idea and another. Ever since my father died, I've worked for wages at one job and the next, but I always come back to the same idea, as if it's waiting for me."

"And what's that?"

I took a deliberate breath and was glad no one else was around to hear me. "I think I'd like to study to be a lawyer. It seems like that's what I should do, what I'm meant to do. Like a calling."

Her eyes were serious and her expression was soft, and I felt as if she was discovering something about me. "That's good," she said. "A profession, like your father."

"It's something I can do on my own," I went on. "That is, I wouldn't need someone to finance me. Of course, I'd have to work, but I could do that while I studied. Then if I had my practice, I could work on my own."

I heard a *pop!* outside, and I looked out the window where the cows had been. The lot was still empty.

"Anyway," I said, "it's an idea." I began to spread jam on the open biscuit.

She nodded. "A good one. You could—"

Her words were cut off by the scrape of the back door opening. Clark came huffing in as he swung the door shut behind him. He set his newspaper on the bar and cleared his throat.

"Sounded like someone fired a shot downtown," he said. "Did you hear it?"

"I just heard a pop," I answered.

"It was louder than that. It was a shot. Sounded like it came from the middle of town." Clark frowned as his eyes drifted over the two of us.

Rachel shrugged, and with her left hand trailing she turned to walk away.

"Thank you," I said. "I'll see you later."

"Thank you." And she gave me a smile that said, yes, she would see me again.

Clark took his seat and put on his spectacles. "One shot, loud and clear," he said. "You know, no one's supposed to fire a gun in town. There's an ordinance."

"I know."

"There's always someone that thinks he doesn't have to follow the law, though."

"That's right," I said. "That's why some people think the town should hire a lawman." I took a bite of the biscuit with jam. The preserves had a tart taste that I knew was plum.

"Ah, hell," said Clark. "Pay someone to sit on his ass? You don't need a lawman just because someone fires a gun. Fine the son of a bitch, I say."

"What if someone gets shot?"

"Oh, well, that's different. By the way, are you goin' back through town?"

"I intend to." I took another bite of the biscuit and jam.

He didn't speak for a moment. I thought he wanted to tell me to come back and report on the disturbance but decided he would rather not owe me a favor. At length he said, "I doubt that it's anything serious. Just one shot. Probably a cowpuncher, or one of them ditch diggers."

By the time I paid my bill and my horse pointed back toward town, a hubbub had arisen. Men were gathering in the street between the saloon and the mercantile, and the muddled sound of voices carried on the air. I did not think Dunbar was in the middle of it, as we had split up only half an hour before. Of course, he might have found Tut Whipple at home, or he might have had a short visit for some other reason, but I still did not think he would have gone downtown that soon and gotten into a scrape. If such things are possible, I did not feel it on the air.

As I rode the next block and a half, I saw no activity at the coal yard, the grain warehouse, the wagon and buggy yard, the blacksmith shop, or the construction of the new bank. A good twenty men had gathered in the street, some in shirt sleeves and bareheaded. I dismounted and led my horse forward.

Up on the sidewalk in front of the mercantile, Fenn Fuller stood in conference with Lon Buckley and Al Redington.

Buckley was wearing a narrow-brimmed hat, while Fuller and Redington looked as if they had come out of their places of business in too much of a hurry to grab a hat. So did Fuller's clerk, who stood off to the side looking pale and stricken.

I searched the crowd for someone I would feel comfortable asking. My eyes hit on Henry Dornick, who stood by in his dusty hat and his loose-fitting clothes. He had a casual air about him as he smoked his curved-stem pipe and chatted with the druggist who owned the parrot.

I moved closer to Dornick and caught his attention.

"Hello, Grey," he said. "Did you just get here?"

"Yes, I did. I was down the street having something to eat, and Clark said he heard a gunshot over this way."

"He was right about that." Dornick blew a cloud of smoke out the side of his mouth.

"Anyone hurt?" I asked.

"Oh, yeah," said Dornick. "Man was killed."

"Really? Who was it?"

"Ben Marston's man, Brownie."

A jolt went through my upper body. "Right here on the street?" I asked.

Dornick took his pipe out of his mouth and said, "Right over there, between Fenn's store and the boarding house. He was in chewin' the fat with Buzzy, and when he came outside, it looks like someone called to him from back in there. When he stepped off the sidewalk, they let him have it."

I looked over at the narrow space between the two buildings and then at Fenn Fuller's clerk, Buzzy. From his sick, pasty expression I guessed that he had been the first one on the scene. I took a steady breath and said, "Any idea who did it?"

The druggist spoke up. "They think it was your friend."

"Dunbar?"

"That's right." The druggist was a short, balding man with

curly gray hair and puffy eyelids. He squinted at me and said, "He threatened to kill him twice."

"I don't think so," I said.

"Lon Buckley said the two of 'em had a run-in a couple of hours earlier, right there in the saloon."

"I was there, and Dunbar didn't threaten him. He told him not to try anything. Pretty much what he told him the time before."

"We'll see," said the druggist. "But we can't have men gettin' ambushed right on Main Street. Someone's got to do something."

"Where's the body?" I asked.

"They took it to the barber shop," said Dornick. He took a puff on his pipe. "Fenn saw to that, first thing."

At that moment, Fuller called out. "Henry, could you come up here?"

"Sure," said Dornick. He nodded to the druggist and me. "Talk to you later."

The druggist turned away in the opposite direction and left me standing with my horse.

The noise of the crowd continued as Henry Dornick joined the other three members of the unofficial town council. Redington had an intent look on his face as he leaned his head forward with his mouth half-open. Fuller was shading his eyes with his left hand, and his high forehead was pink in the sunlight. Lon Buckley, with his chin up, surveyed the crowd as he listened to the others.

The muttering around me began to fall off, and the men shifted position. The conversation on the sidewalk came to a stop as well, and the council members looked up the street just beyond the crowd. All the voices died down, and the men in front of me moved apart as if to make way for something that was coming. Then I could see what the others did. Sauntering down the main street of Winsome on his buckskin horse came Dunbar, his black mustache and hat visible above the dark mane and forelock of the horse. He had tied his canvas coat to the back of the saddle, and he looked trim in his charcoal-colored vest. Ten yards from the edge of the crowd, he dismounted and came the rest of the way on foot.

"Afternoon," he said. "Looks like some kind of a meetin'."

No one spoke, as if each man was waiting for someone else. After an uncomfortable fifteen seconds, Fenn Fuller answered.

"That's right. A man's been killed."

Dunbar frowned. "That's too bad." He glanced at the crowd and then at the men on the sidewalk. "I'd guess you've got the man who did it, or you wouldn't all be standin' around."

"No, we don't," said Fuller. "Not yet. We thought you might be able to tell us something."

"Who knows?" Dunbar shrugged. "I've tried to tell you things before." He let the silence hang for a second and then said, "I've come into this story later than the rest of you, so first off, I'd have to know who the dead man is."

"A fellow named Brownie. I think you know him."

"Or did."

Fuller's eyes tightened. "I wouldn't make so light of it if I were you. Mr. Buckley says you had an altercation with this same man, just a couple of hours ago."

"Don't know that it was an altercation," said Dunbar, surveying the crowd and coming back to Fuller. "I told him not to crowd me, he said he could put a bullet through me, and I told him not to try it."

"We understand you threatened him."

"Hardly so. Grey was there. Ask him."

I took a breath to brace myself as two dozen pairs of eyes turned toward me. "That's how it was," I said. "If Lon says different, I think he heard wrong. His swamper was there, too."

A voice came up from behind me, a voice I knew. "Well, I wasn't in the saloon at ten o'clock this morning, but there was another time I can swear to, and the kid was there as well, when this man threatened to kill the man who's dead now."

The crowd turned to look at Tut Whipple, whose face was flushed as the sunlight caught his blond hair and mustache. To his left, and back a couple of steps, his hired man Falke stood with his thumbs in his gunbelt.

Dunbar answered. "If you're going to tell that story, you should tell the whole thing. Don't leave out the part where the other man grabbed for his gun. As for my threat, I warned him not to draw it. I told him it would be the last thing he ever did. Grey was there, like you said, so call it what you will."

At this point, Fenn Fuller spoke from his eminence on the sidewalk. "Before this goes any further, we could try to clear up a few details about what happened earlier today."

"Fine with me," said Dunbar.

"Very well, then. What did you do after you had this, um, dispute in the Whitepaw Saloon at a little after ten this morning?"

"Grey Wharton and I got on our horses and headed back to the Little Six."

Fuller nodded downward at me and then at Dunbar. "But it's obvious you didn't go there."

"No, we got interrupted."

"Oh, and how was that?"

"As we were ridin' out through the hills, about three miles south of town, someone took a couple of potshots at us."

Fuller gave a look of surprise and turned to me. "Is that right?"

"Yes, it is," I said.

His eyes went back to Dunbar. "And did you get a look at who it was?"

Dunbar shook his head. "No, by the time we got turned around, he was long gone."

"So you came back to town, the two of you?"

"That's right."

"But you didn't stay together."

"No. We split up and agreed to meet in an hour."

Fuller did his maneuver in which he moved his chin forward and looked down his nose. "And you can account for the time you were apart?"

Dunbar moved his head back and forth, as if considering his answer. "Yes, I can, if I'm pressed on it."

"Oh, answer the man!" Whipple barked.

"Go ahead," said Fuller.

Dunbar pursed his lips so that his mustache went up. He glanced from Fuller to Whipple and back, and then he said, "I was at the house where this man lives."

A murmur ran through the crowd, and Whipple blazed red. "Men get killed for that," he said.

"And for other things. Mind your threats."

As the muttering of the crowd rose, Fuller held up his hands. "Quiet!" he called out. "We've got to have order here." When the noise subsided, he turned to Whipple and said, "Tut, keep a hold on yourself, and answer me this. Did you just get here?"

"Yes," he said, almost pouting. Then in a more cooperative tone he said, "Falke and I rode in while you were all talking to this fellow. We came in on this side of town, so I haven't been to my house yet. But you can be sure I'll ask some questions when I do."

"Do you know anything about these shots that were fired out in the hills?"

"I have no idea. We rode in from the west, you know, and from the sounds of it, we would have come along about an hour later."

Fuller seemed to reflect before he turned to Dunbar and said, "It's a likely thought that if Brownie took those shots at you, it would have given you cause to come back and get even."

Dunbar shook his head. "I'll give you back some of your own words. You need reasonable evidence. First, I don't think Brownie had time to hire a horse, pick up a rifle, and get out on the trail ahead of us. Furthermore, the only tracks we saw were from an unshod horse, and any mount he would have hired would have had shoes. You can ask at the livery stable to be sure, but I don't think he left town."

"Then who do you think took those shots at you?"

I stole a look at Falke, who had a blank expression on his face.

Dunbar said, "I don't make accusations ahead of time."

"But you were looking into it when you came back to town," said Fuller.

"You can assume what you want. But I didn't make it this far until just a few minutes ago, and you won't find anyone who can say he saw me here earlier."

"So who do you think shot him?"

Dunbar gave him a direct stare. "I suggested before that you should bring in a lawman to get to the bottom of some of the wrong doings around here."

Redington's voice came blurting out. "We didn't have any trouble until you came."

"Oh, yes, you did," was Dunbar's answer.

Fuller cleared his throat. "Mr. Dunbar, I think we have a memory of the general sequence of things."

Dunbar, who had quickened for a second, was calm again. "When you say 'we,' do you mean you and the butcher there, or do you mean the whole town?"

"Well, um, I don't know that there's much difference."

"Maybe you should ask someone else, then."

"About what?"

"About wrong doings that no one wants to take the trouble to look into."

Fuller rolled his eyes and said, "Was the Little Six losing cattle before you came here? Was that why Higgins brought you in?"

"I'm not talking about rustled cattle."

Fuller's eyes bore down on him. "Then I fail to see it."

"It may be a matter of sight as much as memory, but I'll put it straight and clear. I'm referring to the disappearance of a young girl."

A gasping murmur spread through the crowd, and I felt dazed, detached. It was as if someone had blown a hole in the middle of the day, and a world of dread was visible through the rift. Coils of snakes, rotting bodies, pestilence. As I came back into myself, I heard bits of chatter in a tone of subdued nervousness. "The Mora girl." "The Mexican." "Said she ran away." A couple of men looked at the ground, while two or three others looked off at nothing as they shifted their feet. Falke seemed oblivious, as well he should, but Tut Whipple's face was tense and scowling, and his eyes were narrowed to slits.

"Here, here," came the voice of Fenn Fuller. "Let's get things in order here. Mr. Dunbar, I think you're trying to divert everyone's attention from the problem at hand."

"Think that if you want."

"Then what does this runaway girl have to do with a man being shot in plain daylight?"

Dunbar tipped up his head. "If you don't want to look into it yourselves, and if you don't want to bring in an impartial lawman, then I guess it's up to any man who wants to find out for himself."

Chapter Thirteen

Dunbar and I stood in the street with our horses as the crowd broke up and drifted away. I did not yet know what the man was onto, but I felt it was something bigger than any of the individuals who had been arguing in the main street of Winsome.

"Let's go take a look," Dunbar said. Draping his reins around the neck of the buckskin, he stepped into the saddle.

I mounted up and fell in alongside as he headed west. At the first corner he turned right, and half a block later he turned right again into the alleyway. We rode past clumps of hollyhocks with their tall stalks putting out the last white and pink flowers of the season. As I had been raised not to be inquisitive about other people's affairs, I tried not to look into the areas in back of the butcher shop, the café, and the boarding house. All the same, I saw the back yards strewn with broken crates, cast-off boots, empty bottles—all these in addition to rubbish piles and ash heaps.

Dunbar stopped when we came even with the space between the boarding house and the mercantile. He swung down from his horse and bent over to study the ground. Then he turned and squatted to peer at the four-foot space between the two buildings. I had dismounted as well, so I moved around in back of him to see what I could. It was just a channel of shadow leading to the sidewalk, and beyond that the empty street with the corner of the Whitepaw Saloon visible on the other side.

"Looks different from back here," he said.

"Sure does."

"No tracks to speak of." He waved his hand at the dry grass and hard dirt, then stood up. Handing me his reins, he walked forward by himself. He studied the ground as he went, and when he got to the corner of the boarding house he turned around and came back, shaking his head. I held the reins out to him, and he said, "Not yet." He turned and took another look at the scene. I was about to ask him if he saw something when I realized he was just taking a second look.

We rode back the way we came, following the alleyway to the street. There we turned right and headed north from the center of town. The next half-block had houses, and on the other side of the cross street sat the slaughter house with corrals to the north of it.

The slaughter house was a long building with a breezeway crossing the middle. When we came to that spot, Dunbar swung down and told me to hold the horses. I dismounted and took his reins. As he walked to the breezeway, I stood at the edge of the street, where I could hear the cattle bawling in the corrals. The odor of stockyards hung in the air and mixed with the smell of dust, and for a moment I had the illusion that time had not passed in the town of Winsome, that I was a boy once again, loitering in the street as I waited for my father.

The flies started to bother me, landing first on the backs of my hands and then buzzing around my face. I held both sets of reins in my left hand so I could fan the flies with my right. The horses swished their tails and pulled on the reins. A thump and a commotion came from one of the corrals. Across town, someone was driving nails with a hammer, five raps at a time.

Dunbar came out of the slaughter house with a business-like expression on his face.

"Where now?" I asked.

"Back to talk to our friends. But you know, I think we should water these horses first."

We made the short ride to the town well, where we let the horses drink. Dunbar took off his gloves, put them in his saddle bag, and set his hat on the pommel. Then I worked the pump as he splashed water on his face and rubbed it from his eyes and mustache. I caught a glimpse of the dark spot in his hand, and as we led the horses away from the trough, I noticed he did not put his gloves on again.

After riding from the middle of one block to the middle of the next, we tied up in front of the Whitepaw Saloon. My boots had picked up some damp earth at the water trough, so I paused to scrape my soles on the edge of the sidewalk. Then I followed Dunbar inside, where after closing the door we stood for a moment to let our eyes adjust.

Several men had gathered in the establishment, and I assumed Lon Buckley was enjoying some benefit from having had a killing across the street. Men were standing in groups of two or three along the bar. Above them, the painting of the Indian brave and his conquest seemed to have regained its vitality. In a second glance at the men at the bar, I picked out Whipple and Falke, who faced one another and leaned each with an elbow on the varnished top.

Closer to us and on the right, the council sat at its table. Lon Buckley had his chair pushed back a couple of feet, where he could keep an eye on his business as the meeting went on. The other three men had drinks in front of them, and it looked like a regular gathering for them except Fenn Fuller had not taken off his hat.

With his spurs clinking, Dunbar led the way to their table. Dornick looked at him with interest, while Fuller glanced up and then ignored him. Redington kept his back turned.

"In the interest of truth," said Dunbar, "I'd like a moment of your time."

Redington heaved out a short breath and spoke over his shoulder. "I think we've had enough of your alarms."

A look of amusement spread over Dunbar's face. "Call 'em announcements. But right now I'd just like to share some knowledge."

"Like what?" asked Fuller, with his button nose lifted.

"About someone who was out back of the boarding house a little earlier in the day."

Now he had the attention of all four men at the table as well as some from the bar.

"Well, go ahead," said Fuller.

"A man had his horse tied up about a block north of where the shooting took place. Tied to a fence on the east side of the slaughter house."

"That would be my fence," said Dornick. "That's my yard, where I keep materials."

"I saw the piles of rock and what-not. Anyway, the horse was tied there for about half an hour, and then it was gone."

"What kind of a horse?" asked Redington.

"The color of dirt, as I had it described."

"Bah," said the butcher. "There's a dozen colors of dirt."

"Between gray and light brown, we'll say." Dunbar paused, looked over at the bar, and then addressed the table again. "The man who came for it was a tall man, wearing a tall hat."

Falke slammed his beer mug on the top of the bar. "I'll make you eat those words," he said, in a voice that was loud and not perfectly steady.

Fuller's eyes were intent on Dunbar. "This sounds like a serious accusation," he said.

"No more so than the one you laid on me."

"Well, you were in town, and you had the motive."

"The same goes for someone else."

"Whipple said they had just come into town."

"Of course he did."

Fuller gave a petulant wrinkle of the nose as he sniffed. "Tell me the motive then. And it's got to be more than just to put the blame on you."

"Well, that's part of it. People have reasons to want me out of the way. But I think you know, at least some of you, that this man Brownie was snooping into the past affairs of our ditch contractor."

Lon Buckley's eyes were wide open, and his mouth made the shape of a closed "O," but he said nothing.

"So if you really do want to get at the truth," said Dunbar, "you could ask a question or two of the tall man in the tall hat."

Falke stepped forward from the bar, his six-gun in plain view and his hand hovering over it. "You're a cheeky son of a bitch," he said. "You as much as call me a liar and a killer."

Dunbar raised his eyebrows and tipped his head. "Well, you either were or were not in town, and I've talked to someone who said you were."

"A greaser."

"You sound like Brownie. As for whether you're a killer, you did shoot Tim Odell. You were able to do it in what passed for a fair fight, but you picked it. You know that."

"You're gettin' off the subject. I'm talkin' about Brownie. You as much as say I killed him."

Dunbar tipped his hat toward the table. "These men can verify what I heard, that you were in town. And they may be forming ideas about your motive."

Falke shifted his feet into what I imagined was his position. I moved a few steps to my right.

"I don't like someone callin' me a liar," he said, his words slow and deliberate.

Dunbar held a steady gaze as he answered. "If you live long enough, it won't be the last time. There was a rifle and scabbard tied onto that horse as well."

"So what does that mean?"

"Did you put two more shells in it after you took those shots at me?"

"You're way off the beam. I was nowhere out there."

"Oh, you and the boss say you came in later, but people know better. You were in town before. He waited while you went out and laid for me. You came back and reported to him twice—once when you missed, and once when you didn't."

"Why, you're callin' us both liars."

"Sure, but your boss won't do anything about it as long as he's got you."

Falke's eyes flickered to his right. Whipple had not come forward from the bar.

"I think you should give your gun to Mr. Fuller," said Dunbar, "and answer a few questions."

"Me? When you're the one that—"

"Tell him to go to hell," said Whipple. "We've got nothin' to be afraid of. We know where we were."

"So do others," said Dunbar. "Now hand over your gun."

"You'll have to take it from me."

"I can do that, too." As Dunbar made a move forward, the other man's eyes turned wide and defiant. He drew his gun, but Dunbar jumped to the left and drew his as the shot from Falke's .45 split the air in the saloon. Dunbar fired and caught the man dead center, and the tall hat rolled away as Falke hit the floor.

All the other men in the saloon were on their feet and backed away. Fenn Fuller had a stunned look on his face, while Dornick was craning his neck and taking interest in the man on the floor.

"Things have begun," said Dunbar, "but they're not finished."

"You killed this man," said Fuller.

Dunbar frowned. "Was I supposed to let him shoot me? This is the third time he tried to put me out of the way, if you count settin' me up for shootin' Brownie."

"You seem to be certain about it. Why would he be so urgent?"

"We'll see," said Dunbar. "You could ask his boss, but he won't tell you."

Tut Whipple had been standing silent. Now as the eyes of the saloon turned on him, he burst out. "For God's sake, the man's been killed. Have you got no respect? Someone help me with the body."

No one moved for a second, and then Al Redington stepped away from his group. "I'll go to the barber shop," he said. "They'll get someone here in a minute."

Whipple stood with his hands on his hips, heaving great breaths out through his straw-colored mustache. His face was flushed in turmoil, but he did not look at Dunbar.

Outside, I followed Dunbar to the hitching rail. We untied our horses and led them into the street, where we mounted up. Again we rode west, this time to the second corner, where we turned left. Another block took us to Whipple's yard.

Ruth appeared at the front door, a light figure in the shade, then stepped out and closed the door behind her. She stood waiting, her face tense.

Dunbar and I dismounted and tied our horses. I assumed he had come by earlier to ask about Tut's whereabouts, and I wondered what other questions he might have now.

Ruth did not look at me for more than a second. She kept her eyes on Dunbar, and when we were a couple of yards away, she said, "He's not here. He hasn't come by."

"He's downtown," said Dunbar, "tending to his hired man Falke. There was a shooting."

"I saw a couple of men go by here in a hurry. Who was shot?" Her blue eyes were full of worry as they searched him.

"Actually, there were two. A fellow named Brownie, who worked for Ben Marston, and then Falke."

She expelled a short breath, glanced at me, and brought her eyes back to Dunbar. Her mouth moved with a twitch I hadn't seen before, and then she asked, "Did you come to tell me this?"

"No."

"It's something about Tut, isn't it? Was he in either of the shootings?"

"Not directly. He stood back."

Her eyes would not hold steady, and her voice quavered. "What is it, then?"

"Ruth," he said, "I'm convinced your husband is in deep trouble, and I'm going to ask that the town leaders hold him until they can send for the law."

She gasped, and her face seemed to grow older in a second. "What has he done?" she asked, her voice still shaky.

"It has to do with the disappearance of a girl."

I could see the dread seeping into her just as it spread through me. I wished I was miles away, I wished I could rush to her and hold her, but I was rooted to the spot.

"What girl?" she asked. Her voice was low and steadier now.

"Here, it was a young girl named Annie Mora."

"You say, here."

"There may have been others. Probably were."

Ruth took a deep breath and said, "That's why you came here, to look for her. They sent for you."

Dunbar shook his head. "Nobody sent for me. Quite to the contrary. Fuller and the others were content not to lift a finger. I followed him here."

"Where did the girl end up?"

"She never left town. I'm sure of that."

Ruth's eyes drew close. "Then how did you follow him?"

"Some of this I've heard from you, so you might think I'm saying it back, but it starts in a place you know." Dunbar paused. "You didn't tell me you left North Platte in a hurry."

"Tut was always jumping from place to place. He said the work was no good in North Platte, and he wanted to go to Garden City. I thought one of his business deals went bad."

"Don't rule it out."

Her mouth stiffened as it did when someone other than herself made slighting remarks about her husband.

"At any rate, you went to Garden City, where he worked until he was satisfied there, and then you came here."

"That's right. We stopped in a couple of towns in eastern Colorado, but for only a day or two at a time."

"Well, that's the trail I've been following," said Dunbar. "I've thought you might resent me for bringing him to justice, so I came to tell you before I take the next step."

"Resent you," she said in a rising voice. "I should say I might. You come here gallant and friendly, and all the time you're wheedling me for information to use against him."

"I'm sorry if it seems that way, because it wasn't entirely. And I thought that if I told you some of the story now, you might forgive me at least a little."

"Well, go ahead. It's evident there's no turning back now."

My spirits picked up when she showed that bit of pluck, and I turned to Dunbar to hear what he had to say next.

"It starts in Nebraska," he said. "North Platte. There was a girl, sixteen years old. We'll call her Violet. One night when she had gone out the window to meet a boy who worked in a dry-goods store, she was intercepted by a man. An older man, to her, and a strong one. He threatened to kill her, put a pistol under her jaw, and took her to an old potato cellar. When he had his way with her, he tried strangling her and thought he succeeded. Then while he was digging a hole in the floor of that cellar, she came to and got away."

"And she described him?"

"Not very well. It was dark. She could only say that he was a fully grown man, strong, with a mustache. She was pretty well broken up."

"Did you talk to her?"

"Not directly. I came into this case a little later."

"I see."

Dunbar took a slow breath and went on. "I couldn't turn up anybody in North Platte, and I reasoned that a bungled job such as that one might put a scare into a man. So I asked around for quite a while and got the names and descriptions of men who had left town on short notice. One of those leads took me to Garden City."

"When we were there?"

"No, you had left by then. But not long before you did, a girl of about the same age disappeared."

Ruth's face opened up in a ripple of recognition. "That's right. I remember. They still hadn't found her when we left. Some people said she might have run away."

"I didn't think so when I was there, and even less so now. It was a neater job that time—no witnesses, no body to be found."

"And so you came here."

"I left Kansas, and like you said, I followed the way through eastern Colorado, then up through Cheyenne and on to this town. It was not much of a surprise to learn that a girl had gone missing here as well. But I knew it would hurt my case if I sprang it too soon. So I've pieced together every detail that I could—when the girl disappeared, what Mr. Whipple was doing at that time, what anyone else was doing."

Ruth's face had taken on a deeper expression, which I read

as a mixture of worry and fear.

"It would be difficult for me to contradict any of this," she said, "although it seems so strange. Yet I know it's common for a woman not to know everything about her husband."

"If I weren't so sure of it, I wouldn't be telling you at this point."

"But why?" she asked, her lip trembling. "Why would a man do that when he has—"

She didn't finish her sentence, but I did: a lovely wife at home.

"It's a pattern," said Dunbar. "The people who study these cases, called alienists, have their explanation. They call men like this *psychopaths,* and they say it comes from being self-centered."

"He's all of that."

Dunbar went on. "So self-centered that they have no feeling for another person's pain or suffering. They tend to what they think of as their own needs—to take possession, to silence, and then to keep possession by hoarding the evidence as their own secret."

"My God. And men do this. Of course they do. One reads of it in the papers."

"There was a fellow in Chicago, during the World's Fair, who went through one after another. You know, small-town working girls flocked to that city, and it swallowed them up. No telling how many fell into that man's hands. He had an incinerator. More of an insatiable sort, not like the fellow who plants one in every place he goes."

"He sounds like a maniac."

"Not the same, I grant, except in their being psychopaths. But either way it's a sickness, something that's got to be rooted out. And in this case, the town leaders have protected it without knowing it, or rather by not wanting to know it, like a person with a cancer."

Ruth's eyes were wide, almost wild, and the breeze had put wisps of her hair out of place. "And you say he's that type. I don't know how much to believe."

"I wouldn't expect you to believe it on the basis of my saying it. I've been following a pattern and a chain of reasoning. But as the wise Mr. Fuller keeps saying, there's got to be proof. Evidence."

"And you think you have it, or know where it is?"

Dunbar nodded.

"Then we'll know pretty soon."

"I'd say by morning."

Ruth had been wringing her hands, and now they stopped. She looked full at me for the first time. "Grey, I'm sorry to see you in the middle of this. I hope you'll come and see me when it's, well—"

"I will. Don't worry."

She laughed, almost in a sob. "Not worry. Of course not. I'll just sit here and do my stitchery, like an old crone."

"I'll say again that I'm sorry," said Dunbar. "But come what may, I hope you'll remember that I told you ahead of time."

"I'm sure I will."

I could tell she was put out at him, and I hoped her anger would help her in whatever came next.

After a short good-bye, Dunbar and I mounted up and rode back into town. When we had turned the corner and had put the Whipple residence out of sight, he spoke.

"The sun's not past the yardarm yet, but I think we should put up in town for the night. We can leave the horses at the livery stable and take a room in the boarding house. You don't have any objection, do you?"

"No, not really."

"Good. We can get something to eat while we're at it."

I began to feel like Dunbar's little donkey, but in name at

least he was still working for Higgins, and I felt I should be there not only to bear him company but to report to Higgins in case someone got to Dunbar after all.

I thought he might have had a similar inkling, for we went straight from the livery stable to the boarding house, where we holed up in our room and waited for supper.

Dunbar sat on his cot, trim in his wool vest, and faced me as I sat on mine. I could tell he wanted to say something, so I waited for him to speak.

"That was a rough visit," he said. "I think we put Mrs. Whipple through a hard time. Even at that, there's things you can't say to a woman, especially to someone's wife, but there are facts to the case that are even uglier."

I nodded, though I was not sure how much I wanted to hear.

"This whole idea of takin' possession. You know, it's not just the act, like you'd think a caveman would do."

"Oh."

"There's a part where he tells the victim, to be sure she knows."

"You heard this from—"

"Violet? No, I read it in her testimony. But it gives you an idea of what the final minutes might be like."

A chill went across my shoulders and neck.

He went on. "As Violet told it, the man whispered in her ear that she had to smell him, feel him, take his seed inside her, and then know that she had done that and still had him in her. That's how he keeps possession, with her knowing and after that with his deposit."

I let out a long breath. I felt washed out, all in a moment, though it might have been an accumulation of everything that had happened that day.

"Sorry," he said. "It's ugly, like I said. You can see why I couldn't tell her, and maybe I shouldn't have told you."

"No harm, I guess."

"Maybe not. Everyone calls you a kid, but I think you're old enough to know about some of the rottenness in life and make your own judgments."

I shrugged.

"Well, it's the truth, at least."

After that we stretched out on our cots and didn't say anything until the supper bell rang.

After supper we went back to our room, where I lay staring at the ceiling once again. Dunbar did the same and did not interrupt me. I thought of Ruth, eaten up by worry, and I wondered whether Tut had taken refuge in his house or had gone out to the work camp. I pictured Brownie and Falke, lying in the dark in the back of the barber shop. I thought of Fenn Fuller and doubted that his nerves were as keyed up as mine were, though I assumed he had his worries about what was yet to come. Then I put myself through the ordeal of imagining the terror of Annie Mora, the nameless girl in Garden City, and the girl in North Platte who was referred to as Violet. I was sick in my guts, and I had no pity for what might happen to Tut Whipple.

When the lamp was turned off, I lay for another long while. I was a jangled mess of dread, fatigue, and restlessness. I did not think I would be able to sleep that night, but at some point I dropped off.

At well past midnight I awoke. It was too quiet in the room. Moonlight came in through the thin curtains, enough for me to see that Dunbar's bed was empty. I told myself that wherever he had gone was not my worry. Not now. Not until morning.

Chapter Fourteen

I was sitting at the breakfast table of the boarding house trying to fortify myself with hotcakes and bacon when I heard the fire bell. I pushed away from the table, grabbed my hat off the hook, and ran out into the gray morning.

It was early, not much after sunrise, and daylight straggled through a gloomy cloud cover. The bell was clanging and men came running, some carrying buckets and others pulling on coats or holding onto their hats. I made the short run to the corner where the bell sat in front of the blacksmith shop. Men were gathering, and I couldn't see what was the cause of alarm until I picked out the dark hat of Dunbar.

Amidst the calls of "What is it? What is it?" came the muttering of a different tone. "It's gone." "No water." The men in front of me shifted. A couple of them ran forward a few steps. More muttering. Then my field of vision opened, and I saw that the surface of the pond was gone. From where I stood I could see only a bed of mud.

The bell went silent. Men were still arriving but slower now, as the crowd was not moving. Voices rose and fell. "What is it?" "What happened?" "Where's the fire?" "Where's the water gone?" Then someone said, "Here comes Fuller."

I turned to see the storekeeper marching forward. He had his coat buttoned up and his hat in place, and he was swinging his elbows as he came to take command.

"What's going on?" he barked.

Men crowded aside to clear the way between the man in the bowler and spectacles and the man in the large-crowned hat and mustache.

"What is going on?" demanded Fuller, enunciating his syllables as he faced Dunbar.

"Time to stand behind your words."

"What do you mean?"

"You said that if the town had a problem, you'd see to it."

I thought Fuller was going to explode. "You *make* problems," he said as his chest rose. "You killed a man in the saloon, you may have killed another before that, and now you've ruined our reservoir."

"I didn't ruin it. I just wanted you to see something. You and the others."

"And that's the way to get our attention?"

"Come along, then." Dunbar turned and walked toward the street that ran downhill to the bridge. I saw then that he was carrying a shovel.

Fuller pushed ahead as the crowd moved along the street. A few men had already gone onto the dam itself and were peering down both sides.

Halfway down the slope, Dunbar stopped and turned around. The mass of men stopped. I moved to the front so I could see better, and I drew back at the sight.

All of the retaining boards had been pulled out of the headgate and lay on the top of the earthen mound. To the right of the wooden structure, a breach had been cut in the dam itself, and below the gate, silt and light debris covered the rocks of the spillway. I could see that Dunbar had drained the pond to the bottom of the headgate, or weir, and then made the cut to drain the water the rest of the way down. He had done a neat job of it.

"You've got no right to do this," said Fuller, bristling in his side-whiskers. "It's a violation."

"Get a shovel yourself." Dunbar looked around. "All of you. Put away your buckets and get shovels."

"To wreck it some more?"

"No, you fool. To dig."

The voices picked up again, and men began moving aside. I turned to see two men on horseback coming down the hill. I recognized them at the same time—Whipple on a sorrel horse, and his toady Stiver on the yellowish-white plug that he rode. Whipple's tan hat rose in the gray sky, and a little lower than it, Stiver's billed cap stuck up like a muffin.

"Hold it there!" Whipple called out.

Dunbar kept his eyes on the two men as the horses came slow-footing and stopped.

"You're not going to do any more," said Whipple, his voice still loud.

In that instant, Stiver swung off his horse and came into view with his gun drawn. He fired twice at Dunbar, who still had the shovel in his left hand as he drew his gun with his right and fired.

Stiver lurched as a red spot appeared between his brown suspenders. He doubled over, dropped his pistol in front of him, and fell to the side. The white horse ran off, and Whipple fought with the reins to keep the sorrel from doing the same.

When the horse settled down, Dunbar had Whipple covered. "That didn't work," he said.

Whipple still had fire in his eyes, and his firm mustache gave him an air of authority. "Unless you want to shoot every man here, you're not going to undo any more of my work."

Dunbar kept his eyes square on the man as he said, "Some of it can't be undone. But if I have to shoot someone else, I'll start with you. Just go for your gun, and you'll see."

I knew Tut Whipple well enough to know that he wouldn't

take a fight that he might lose. So I wasn't surprised when he eased down from the saddle and took off his gunbelt. He rolled it up and stuffed it in the saddle bag, then turned around.

"Shoot me now," he said.

"I didn't come for that," said Dunbar as he put the .45 in his holster.

"Then take off yours."

Dunbar unbuckled his belt, motioned to me, and held out the holster, gun, and belt. I took the set, and as I stepped back, I noticed that he had taken off his vest at some earlier moment. He had taken off his spurs the night before and had not put them back on.

Dunbar held the shovel upright with the point of it on the ground. "I came to dig," he said. "And to get the men of the town to dig."

Whipple was breathing hard. His face showed agitation, and his eyes flickered at the wall of dirt.

"You men," said Dunbar, "and you, Fuller. If you don't believe me and don't want to lift a finger, Grey and I'll do it all ourselves. It'll just take longer, that's all." He hefted his shovel and said to me, "Go set that outfit where it won't get dirt on it, and get one of these."

Whipple went into a fury. He charged Dunbar, who had time to toss the shovel aside but not to get out of the way. Whipple let out a savage cry of "Aargh!" as he rammed his shoulder into Dunbar's abdomen. Both men's hats went tumbling aside as the blond-headed man locked his arms around the dark-haired one and drove him to the earth.

They rolled across the slope and downward, out of sight for an instant. I saw only the base of the dam and the rocks I had put there, and two or three seconds drew out into a suspended moment. I saw the mound of dirt, and the rocks. I remembered how we had laid that base, day by day, and how I had quit the job after we put in the headgate. Now I saw the whole picture—how Whipple had made his deposit in the girl's body, then buried her in the midst of all of us, a deposit within a deposit. And I had helped. We all had. I had moved dirt and placed the rocks. Others had done their part—even Fuller, who never touched a shovel, and the little boys who threw empty bottles into the water when the pond had filled.

The light hair and dark hair came into view as the two men rose to their feet. Whipple swung a fist into the side of Dunbar's head, setting him back on his feet. Whipple rushed again, and Dunbar glanced a blow off the man's right cheekbone. Whipple crouched and grabbed Dunbar's leg, then raised it. Dunbar hopped on his left foot, swung a left hook at Whipple's temple, and spilled aside. The two men scrambled and came up, only to hit the ground again as Whipple tackled his enemy.

Now they wrestled on the grassy slope, each locked in the other's iron grip, each driving a short punch at the other's head whenever he had the clearance. The struggle took them to a level spot not far from the stone bridge, where they came to a momentary stop with Whipple's right arm clasped across Dunbar's throat. He tightened it like a vise, and with his left hand he reached over Dunbar's head and clawed at the man's upper cheek and eye.

Dunbar thrashed, then with a tremendous burst of force broke free. He rolled over to one side, and as he was coming up on all fours, Whipple rushed him again.

I could see that Whipple did not want to fight with his fists any more than he wanted to fight with a gun. He had seen how others had fared. Keeping at close quarters was his best chance, and he was doing all right at it. He had knocked the other man down and had a hold on him. He settled both hands on Dunbar's throat, held down with all his weight, and stepped over to straddle his opponent. Then he lowered himself to sit on

Dunbar's chest and ribs.

This is it, I thought. *This is how he does it.*

Dunbar gave a new burst of energy and threw Whipple off balance. The shock of blond hair shook as Dunbar's fist came into view, skidding off Whipple's chin. The two men rolled again, and Dunbar came up with his back to me. Whipple rose in front of him, and Dunbar slugged the man on the jaw. With the same cry of rage as before, Whipple lowered his head and charged. Dunbar sprawled and pushed the man's head downward, but Whipple got hold of a leg and pulled Dunbar off his balance.

They tumbled to the spillway, and this time Whipple got his left hand around Dunbar's neck. With his right hand he grabbed a rock that filled his grasp. He lifted it, and as he brought it down, Dunbar twisted aside and threw Whipple off balance. The rock went rattling on the others, and Dunbar broke free.

He stood up, and as Whipple came to his feet, Dunbar slammed him with three punches in a row. Whipple bent to pick up another rock, and Dunbar caught him with an uppercut. The blond head snapped up and back, and for a second Whipple stood straight and still. Dunbar backed him up with two more solid punches, then finished him with a powerful left cross that sent him falling backward. Whipple's head bounced off the edge of the stone bridge, and he fell to his side and lay still.

Dunbar moved back a few steps. Whipple did not move. Redington emerged from the group of men behind me, and with Fuller pushing him, he walked toward the body.

"Tut," he said. "Are you all done?" He exchanged a look with Fuller, then went the rest of the way and crouched. His mouth was open as he leaned his bulk forward and reached to touch the man. Half a minute later he turned and said, "He's dead."

As a rumble of voices broke out around me, I let out a long breath. I felt exhausted, and my mouth was dry. Though I was wearing my hat and jacket, I shivered.

Dunbar was standing off by himself, breathing hard and wiping his cuff on his cheekbone. He was scraped and bruised and dirty, but he stood up straight.

Fuller's voice rose on the air, sharp and demanding. "Where does this end?"

"Right here," said Dunbar, pointing at the base of the dam. "Get some shovels, unless you're afraid. I think you know what you'll find."

Henry Dornick stepped from the crowd, dressed for work in his dusty hat and loose clothes. "I'll get a shovel," he said. "I'll use this one." He picked up the shovel that had fallen aside in the fight.

Fuller's eyes were hard and narrow behind his spectacles as his gaze flickered from Dunbar to the mound of dirt. Without a word he turned away, and Redington followed him up the hill.

Dornick held the shovel upright at his side like a staff. He faced the men in the crowd and swept his glance up to the men who stood on top of the mound. His voice rose clear in the dull morning. "I say we dig. Every man who's got a shovel and isn't afraid of a little work, go get it."

I waited for Dunbar to retrieve his hat, and then I handed him his gunbelt.

"Thanks," he said. After he buckled on the belt, he worked his right hand. As he opened his fist and closed it, I saw the dark brand. "None of this is easy," he went on, still taking deep breaths. "But it's close to done." He shook his head and worked the hand again. "I need to go get cleaned up. I'll find you in a little while."

I lingered as he walked up the slope, not limping but with a wincing, shifting gait that showed he had taken a beating.

Dornick took a position on top of the dam, and men from

the town began to arrive with shovels. I wondered if I, too, should dig, and then I realized someone should go tell Ruth.

It was not a long walk, but it did me good to warm up a little and get rid of some of the tension. When I knocked at Ruth's door, she opened right away, and from the lost expression on her face I could tell she had already heard the news.

"Ruth," I began.

"I know, Grey. Mr. Fuller sent his clerk." She stepped aside and let me in.

"I'm sorry for you," I said as I took off my hat.

Her blond hair was disheveled as she shook her head. "Oh, it can't be helped."

"Tut was desperate. He knew it was up, but he tried to stop it anyway. In the end, it was all or nothing for him."

She shook her head again. "It was nothing. All he had left was nothing. He knew it, and still he tried to beat it."

My thoughts drifted back, and I said, "I wonder how long he knew."

Ruth blinked her eyes and brushed aside a wisp of hair. "Who knows?"

"I wonder if, deep down, he knew it but wouldn't admit it to himself."

"Knew what? That he would be caught?"

"More than that. I wonder if he knew all along, in some way, that the stranger had come for him. It almost seems as if he did."

"He kept a great deal to himself. We know that now."

I rotated my hat in my hands. "Is there anything you'd like me to do for you?"

She forced a smile. "Why don't you just sit for a while? You don't have to say anything. Just sit here in the same room."

"I can do that."

She took a seat at one end of the couch, and I sat at the other. I could hear her breathing and the clock ticking. In the midst of this stillness, I thought of the commotion at the other end of town. I imagined men taking away the bodies of Stiver and Whipple while others dug in the muck. The clock ticked, and time dragged on.

Almost an hour had passed when I heard the footfalls of a horse. A minute later, a knock came at the door. I rose to my feet as Ruth went to the door and opened it.

There stood Dunbar with his hat in his hand, looking better than the last time I had seen him. He had a scrape on his forehead and a bruise on his cheek, but he had washed his face and brushed the dirt off his clothes. He had also put on his vest and spurs.

"Come in," said Ruth.

"Thank you." As he stepped inside he said, "Hello, Grey."

I nodded, then turned to Ruth and said, "I guess I should be going now." I started for the couch where I had left my hat.

"Not yet," said Dunbar. "I won't be long. I didn't mean to interrupt."

"Interrupt?" cried Ruth, raising her eyes to him. "After everything else?"

"I'm sorry," he answered. "In this last part, he gave me no choice. And before that, I did what I had to."

Tears started in her eyes, and her voice was trembling. "You've laid everything to waste here. You came in like a knight, and you leave like a Tartar or a Hun."

"It didn't begin with me."

Now she broke down. She sobbed and sniffled and wiped away the tears. "I could have loved you," she said.

His face fell. "And I could have loved you, if things had been way different. But things are impossible now. You can see that. And really, they would have been impossible if all I had done was ruin him."

"Ruin him?"

"As I intended. Have him handed over to the law. But even then, there would have always been that knowledge, that fact, between us."

Her blue eyes were swimming in torment as she moved her head back and forth. "We might have gotten along."

"No," he said. "I might have thought so, too, but we had no future from the beginning. I knew I had to expose him, but I let myself think that you and I could develop an interest between us. That was my mistake, my error. When the time came closer, I knew that setting things right with Violet and the others was the most important thing of all. And I knew that to do that, I could never come back to you except as I do now. To say good-bye."

She looked at him as if she, too, had seen a stranger. "Then that's all there is," she said.

"That's all. Good-bye, Ruth. And may life treat you better."

"Good-bye."

I thought she was going to say more, and it seemed as if he thought so, too, but after a couple of seconds he nodded and left. She held her head up, and I could see she was gathering her pride.

When the door closed, Ruth and I stood facing each other in the middle of the room. I thought she was holding together rather well when she said, "You didn't have to see that, but I suppose it's all for the better."

"I'm sorry," I said.

"Oh, please, please. There's been too much to be sorry for. Way too much. I've spent my life saying I'm sorry, and now I know what it sounds like."

I was about to say it again, but I held my tongue. I stared at her, and as her face clouded up, I moved toward her and put my arms around her. She let loose with a sob, then a series of smaller ones as she cried into my shoulder. I held my arms around her, I moved my hand to the back of her head, and I pressed her to me.

I don't know if I was in a daze, in a swoon, or under the spell of a strange spirit within me. In a moment of abandon, I said, "I love you, Ruth," and I could not stop there.

"Oh, thank you," she sobbed.

"I love you," I said again. "I'll do anything for you."

"Oh, you don't have to. It's just that everything—"

Now my recklessness swept through me. I let go of her and lowered myself to my knees. I held her upper legs in my arms as I laid my head against the hollow of her hip. "Let me take care of you," I pleaded. "Come with me. Nothing will ever touch you." I felt as if I floated in a separate world, as if a crack or flaw had opened in me and the unguarded desire came welling out and took me with it. What I was saying seemed to come of its own will, and I had the sensation of standing by watching and hearing myself say it. Her voice brought me back.

"No," she said, holding my head away from her. "You can't."

"Yes, I can. You're not that much older."

"It's not just that." She lifted me, and I stood facing her. She took a moment to study me and to pick her words, I suppose. "You need to start a life clean with someone else," she went on, "and not live under the dead hand of the past."

"I don't want to. I want to be with you."

Sad and smiling, she shook her head. "For now you do, but it would be no good for you."

The gash within me began to close, and the strangeness receded like a spirit. I searched her face, so lovely to me. "And you?"

"I'll go my own way and find a new life."

"What I mean is, would it be no good for you?"

She held my face in her hands. "Oh, I can't say. But I know. If you care for me, and I know you do, you'll honor my wish, and we'll all come out of this for the better."

I thought this was brave talk after the position she had taken with Dunbar, yet I told myself that what she said was right. She had pulled herself together after that weak moment. The desire was still surging through me, and more than anything I wanted to kiss her, but she put up a wall of glass as she lowered her hands and stepped back.

She took a steady breath and said, "That's probably enough for now. You're a dear boy, Grey, and I'll never forget what you've meant to me. And now if you'll excuse me, I think I'd better get some clothes for him to be buried in."

My spirits sank, but I did as she asked. I was still in a daze as I put on my hat and walked out into the world. The overcast sky had not lifted, and the dull sound of my steps was the only thing I heard as I walked toward the main street. I wandered across town, and as I approached the corner across from the blacksmith shop, I heard voices. I turned onto the street that had been the scene of all the havoc earlier.

More than a dozen men were at work under the supervision of Dornick, who stood by the spillway and puffed on his curved-stem pipe. Two men had pulled out the headgate with a team of horses and were unhooking the chains. The others were digging on the sides and top of the mound of earth, while at least a dozen townsmen stood by watching. I saw that there were more than enough to do the work, and I did not enjoy the curiosity that hung in the air.

I cast my eyes over the wreckage, greater now than an hour earlier. As far as the dirt and water were concerned, I imagined they could be put together as they were before. As for the things that had happened, I knew none of them could be changed. The merchants could go back to conducting their daily business, but as Dunbar had said, there were things that could not be undone.

I pulled my jacket close and walked up the hill. I went to the boarding house and the livery stable, where I found that Dunbar had paid the bills. It was still early in the day, so I saddled the brown horse and headed back to the ranch to see what turn things would take with Dunbar.

Chapter Fifteen

They found Annie Mora later that morning, at the bottom of the mound of dirt where Tut Whipple thought he had her hidden for good. By then I had left for the ranch.

By the time I got there, Dunbar had packed his gear and was loading it onto the buckskin. The blue roan was already saddled and ready to go, tied to the next hitching rail over. I put my horse away and went into the cook shack, where I found Manfred and Higgins in conference.

"I suppose you got the story," I said.

"We did," said Higgins. "And I guess I've got no complaint, except I've got to rustle up yet one more hand before the wagon pulls out. I'm supposed to have one comin', but I don't know where I'll get the other."

Manfred stroked his chin beard. "We'll get by," he said. Then turning to me, he lifted his brows and made his face look even longer. "Glad to see you home in one piece."

"Glad to be here. There were a few rough moments."

Higgins nodded, drew his mouth together, and said, "You can go help Gene with the wagon."

"All right." I went outside and saw that Dunbar was tying down the canvas cover on his load. I walked over and waited as he tied off the rope.

"Pullin' out?" I said.

"It's time."

I looked down and scuffed the dirt. "I suppose."

"I wish things could have been easier," he said, "but they weren't."

I shook my head and looked up at him. "I couldn't have done things any different, that's for sure. None of it was in my hands."

He untied the roan, led it by the reins, and stopped at the other hitching rail, where he pulled the slip knot on the packhorse's lead rope. He turned both horses around, then stopped to face me as he put on his gloves. He was wearing his canvas coat, and he looked like a packer ready for the trail. "If you've got any questions, now's the time to ask 'em," he said.

I had a few, but only one that I thought would do. "Are you a Pinkerton man?"

"No, I work on my own."

I held out my hand, and he did the same. "So long," I said, "it's been good to know you."

"The same here." He turned the roan into position, and with the lead rope in his right hand he grabbed the saddle horn with his left and pulled himself up into the seat. With the reins in his gloved hand, he turned the roan to the left. As he did so, he raised the lead rope and touched his right hand to the brim of his hat. "So long, Grey. May your pony never stumble."

I stood there for a long moment and watched him ride away on the shadowy grassland. He was heading north, where the wild geese and then the winter storms would come from. I fancied that he was going back to his own origin, a land where men gave up their worldly desires and pondered higher laws of justice, truth, and self-denial.

All of that was twenty years ago. I punched cows for Hig and the Little Six for the rest of that season, and then I studied law. I came back to Winsome and was glad there was no railroad to fight with. There have been other contentious cases, but my pony hasn't stumbled—at least not yet. Rachel and I have made a good life, and it has sealed that flaw in me as much as I can imagine is possible. From time to time we ride out to Decker Rim, where I still see the scars of the reservoir project that was never finished. About once a month we light a candle for Annie Mora, and when I am on my own I sometimes think of those other two, that man and that woman, and how they held up when life broke open.

ABOUT THE AUTHOR

John D. Nesbitt lives in the plains country of Wyoming, where he teaches English and Spanish at Eastern Wyoming College. His published work includes more than thirty books of traditional western, contemporary, mystery, and retro/noir fiction. John has won many awards for his work, including two awards from the Wyoming State Historical Society (for fiction), two awards from Wyoming Writers for encouragement of other writers and service to the organization, two Wyoming Arts Council literary fellowships, a Western Writers of America Spur finalist award for his western novel *Raven Springs,* and the Spur award itself for his noir short story "At the End of the Orchard" and for his western novels *Trouble at the Redstone* and *Stranger in Thunder Basin.* See his website at www.johndnesbitt.com.